D ⊃Y ME

THE LAST VOCARI: BOOK 4

ELENA LAWSON

THORN HOUSE
PUBLISHING

"*I*f you take any more, I'm going to need another burger. Or twelve," I grumbled between mouthfuls, a greasy double bacon and cheddar in one hand while the other lay limp against the table, an IV needle jabbed into the crook of my elbow.

"Just a little more," Ethan said in a tone that was trying way too hard to sound detached. Though I clearly saw him flinch at my remark.

He'd gotten good at dealing with my blood. Before, I could see the discomfort in the lines on his face. The tension between his brows, the slight downturn of his full lips. His bloodthirst made his job of playing doctor and scientist much harder than it needed to be. But now...now he seemed unaffected.

I swallowed another mammoth size bite and set my burger down, trading it in for fries drenched in gravy and cheese curds. These Canadians really knew what they were doing with this poutine shit. It was like crack, even though I could feel my stomach rebelling against the sheer amount of grease and dairy. I couldn't stop eating it. "You're getting really good at that," I told Ethan as he pressed a cotton ball to the base of the IV and gently slid it out from my vein.

Guiding my arm up and into a bent position to staunch the blood flow, he allowed himself a small smirk. "Thinking you could be dead really put things into perspective."

My brows furrowed.

He bit his lower lip. "Your blood doesn't bother me anymore," he explained. "It hasn't since I peeled you off the pavement in NYC."

I offered an impish returning grin as he wheeled himself away, placing the newly filled blood bag with the stack of others in the mini fridge. I could hardly believe it'd already been a week since then. A week since I escaped a building of nearly two hundred vampires.

A week since I escaped Raphael.

I'd slept the first thirty hours after my return, dead to the world in an apartment ringed in a heavy line of salt and black ash to protect us against Amala's magic. When I finally woke, everything was already in motion. Bags packed. Private plane fueled and ready for take-off.

We moved quickly, my three guys and me. Under Azrael's instruction, we made for the tarmac, following the exact route he laid out for us. When we got to the airstrip, we found there were two planes. Well, one was a jet, really. The guys and I took that one, and the other was piloted by and filled with 172 vampires. *Our* army.

Estelle was already on our jet, waiting with a thermos of her famous chicken soup and a warm smile. I had no idea how Azrael had managed it, but I was immeasurably glad to see her. And the soup was just the thing I needed to set my mind back in motion.

"Az will be here soon," Ethan said as he worked, filling vials with blood, bringing me back to the here and now.

I stiffened and his hand paused over a vial, sensing the shift in the atmosphere.

Ethan turned from the long stainless-steel counter so I could see the tight set in his jaw. His caramel hair seemed to have grown while I was gone and dropped low over his brow now, concealing his steeped-tea eyes in shadow. "Are you ever going to tell us what happened in there, Rose?"

I sighed, hopping down from the stool, my appetite suddenly vanished. "It doesn't matter. It's over now."

Ethan's lips pressed into a hard line, but he said nothing, resuming his work. If it had been Frost or Blake, I'd have had to put up more of a fight to make them drop it. But Ethan would never make me talk about something I didn't want to. He'd never make me do *anything* I didn't want to. It was one of the many reasons I loved him so much.

Even if I was doing a piss poor job of showing it lately.

I moved to leave, but in the blink of an eye, Ethan was up and across the floor, his hand wrapping around my wrist to jerk me to a stop. He swallowed my short gasp of surprise with a kiss, fingers pressed to the nape of my neck as he guided my mouth open and dove in with his tongue, stealing all the breath from my lungs.

At first, I was all hard edges. Clenched. The vivid memory of Rafe's fingers on my body flashing before my closed eyelids.

And then...the memory faded.

There was only Ethan.

I shuddered against him, a heavy moan curling up from my chest to be smothered between our lips.

Fuck.

He pulled away, gazing heavily into my eyes as he pressed his forehead against mine. "Sorry," he breathed. "I couldn't wait any longer, it was driving me insane and you didn't stop me so—"

I silenced him with another kiss. This one shorter, but every ounce as toe-curling as the first. I hadn't been intimate with any of my guys since my return. My body was battered and broken then. Healing.

Though the physical things healed in the thirty-odd hours I'd slept, it was my mind that was still fractured. Reeling from the two days spent in a tiny dark box, forced to relive my most painful childhood memory over and over *and over*.

My skin bristled and I bit my lower lip to try to shock the memories away with a stab of pain. It worked, if only for a second.

"Come to bed soon?" I whispered as Ethan pushed my long black hair from my face, brushing it behind my right shoulder.

His brow raised questioningly.

In answer, I dipped my hand down between us grabbing him by his massive cock through his grey sweatpants. He stilled, lips parting at the contact, already growing hard beneath my fingers. How the hell had I waited an entire fucking week to touch them?

What was wrong with me?

If it was a distraction I wanted, I could think of nothing better than being with my guys. I just wasn't sure if I could do it. If I could be *into* it with the shit-storm going on in my brain. I'd been wrong. *Very* wrong.

And I was damn glad to be. Already I could feel my pussy growing damp beneath my fighting leathers and had to press my thighs together to quell the slight burn. Otherwise, I'd wind up letting him take me right here in the lab surrounded by combustible material, blood, and chemicals.

Ethan groaned and I released him.

"Back to work," I ordered with a wink as I spun to leave the room before I could change my mind, sternly reminding myself he had much more important things he needed to be doing.

"The sooner you finish, the sooner..." I trailed off, giggling when I turned to find him piping blood into vials faster than a machine ever could. At this rate he'd be done making two hundred doses of 'Rose's Vampire Sunblock Tattoo Ink'; the name was a work-in-progress, within the hour.

Good, because the things I planned to do to him, to all of them, would take most of the night.

The underground military bunker was buzzing with life at this time of the night. Even though this wing was mostly sealed off from the main barracks along with other rooms where the now-193 vampires were staying, I could still feel them through the walls.

My senses had been somewhat diminished over the past months. Before, when I still hunted them for sport, I never questioned my abilities. Now that prickle of unease that always warned me a vampire was near had all but gone. I blamed spending too much time fucking their kind now instead of staking them, but regardless, I needed to get my shit in order.

With a little active focus though, I found the sixth sense was still there. Like an icy finger on the back of my neck, making the small hairs on my arms and the back of my neck prickle. All of my senses on high alert. Sound flooded my ear canals and if I listened *very* closely, I could hear them through two feet of concrete.

The indecipherable buzz of conversation. A thud and ensuing crack of stone when one vamp got a little too tired of another's bullshit. If anything, that was one of the harder parts of keeping an army of vampires at your disposal—making sure they didn't kill each other.

Second only to keeping them fed.

It didn't help that their promise of meeting the sun had yet to be fulfilled. They were getting impatient. Agitated. Many of them wanted to stand against Raphael, having been turned against their will, with human families they no longer saw but wanted to keep from harm. But many others still hadn't a care in the world for mortal life. They joined only for the promise of sunlight.

Without it, they would desert us faster than I could blink.

I'd be lying if I said every instinct in my body wasn't vibrating with the need to fucking stake each and every one of them. Or at the very least, the ones who would turn on us, if even moderately provoked.

I'd learned not all vampires were the same. My guys had taught me that. To some extent, Azrael had as well. I gulped, shaking my head to cast out that last thought. My mind was enough of a mess without thinking of *him* right now.

If I had any luck, I'd be able to avoid him when he came. I hadn't had to see him since that night in New York, in the apartment building. He saw only the guys. Communicated only by phone. I had no idea if he was doing it *for* me, or because he couldn't stand the sight of me after knowing his brother had put his hands on me. That I'd broken under the weight of them.

The overhead lights blinked, and distantly I heard the generator chug and then resume a rumbling monotone. I had no idea how Azrael had come to own such a place. The bunker was old but had clearly been retrofitted with modern amenities.

The lab was small but had all the top gear a budding scientist could want. When Ethan first saw it, I swear his pupils dilated to conceal all the muted brown tones of his irises.

Frost and Blake liked to spend their time in the gym, which, I assumed, was where I'd find them now. Blowing off steam day in and day out to keep from losing their shit.

Maybe a little *Rose time* would help them chill the fuck out. I could hardly stand to be around them lately. My own edginess heightened whenever forced to bear the weight of theirs as well.

We had maybe another week here before it would be time to act. A week to get everything lined up. To give the army of vampires their promised taste of sunlight. To get them briefed and trained. To come up with a solid plan of attack.

We knew it was only a matter of time before Amala found us here. The blanket of salt and ash atop the bunker wouldn't hold out forever, and even if it did, there were stronger forms of magic which could penetrate it. We were banking on Amala not being able to use them, though. If what Az told the guys was right, then Amala would need a group of witches to perform the spell strong enough to get through our wards—and she always worked alone.

It would take time for her to gather the necessary number of witches to aid her, and none of us thought any even *would* help her at all. The witches wanted Raphael and everything he stood for obliterated just as much as we did. If we were right, *none* would help her.

If we were wrong…

I shuddered, more from the thought than the underground chill constantly clinging to the concrete walls. I didn't want to know what would happen if we were wrong, that was why we needed to be swift. Be smart.

No place was safe for long.

Ahead, the grunts of Blake and Frost were audible, echoing beyond the heavy metal door leading to the gym. I inhaled, a smile pulling at the corner of my mouth. They were my sunshine. Stuck thirty feet below ground, they were the only light in this perpetual dark. I hadn't allowed myself to realize that until Ethan kissed me.

I'd been training, attacking practice dummies with feral rage, since we got here. Eating in silence with the guys. Sleeping alone.

It was time to put an end to it.

My hand closed around the handle when a familiar prickle of unease rushed down my back, making my insides twist and my knees grow weak.

I spun, taking him in.

Azrael stood fifteen feet away down the hall, his expression blank. Eyes slightly unfocused. I could only make out half of his face. He stood in the shadows, where one of the overhead lights were out.

My throat went dry as I took in the tight line of his jaw. The hollow dip below his Adam's apple, just visible over the unbuttoned top of his fitted black dress shirt.

When I finally forced myself to look him in the eyes, making my own to adjust to the shadows, my stomach dropped. In them, I saw Rafe.

Adrenaline flooded my veins, making my fingertips tremble.

I am the motherfucking Black Rose. I do not *tremble.*

I clenched my fists.

"Azrael," I said, keeping my voice level, giving him a slight nod.

He cocked his head, and for the smallest heartbeat, I thought I was wrong. I thought it *was* Rafe. That he'd already found us. That he'd come to kill me himself.

When Azrael took a step forward and I flinched, hand edging down toward the stake strapped to my thigh, he stopped. "You don't have to do that," he said in a low whisper, gaze darting to the closed-door beside me. He was speaking quietly so as not to alert the guys to his presence.

"Do what?" I asked, more certain by the second it was Azrael. There was a menace in his ancient gaze, but not the same darkness as his brother.

His lips pursed slightly, as though tasting something

sour. "Pretend you can stand the sight of me. I know what my brother did."

A vein in his neck pulsed, growing in thickness as he shoved his hands into the pockets of his designer denim, trying to conceal how his hands were stiff with rage. Fingers curving slightly into talons.

"But you aren't him," I ventured, unsure if I spoke the words more for my own benefit or more for his.

Resolved, I lifted my chin and bit the inside of my cheek, striding to him with purpose. My heart a jackhammer beneath the cage of my ribs.

I wouldn't let Rafe do this to me. I wouldn't let that fucking bastard win. There was fear within though, I was loathe to admit that fact, there was something else, too. Something I could use.

Rage.

Rage beyond anything I'd ever felt for another being in my entire life.

Fear was all but useless. But rage…

We were old friends.

As I neared him, I noticed something had been changed. As my vision adjusted to the shadows and Azrael took a minuscule step toward me, I saw that he looked different.

"What did you do?" I asked, falling back a step to get a better look.

Azrael lifted his hand to run his fingers through his freshly cut hair. His near shoulder-length russet brown locks had been cut to stand several inches from his scalp on top, cut shorter on the sides. He wore it pushed back on top and the natural wave of it made it look somehow like it was both styled and effortlessly undone.

I didn't realize I was grinning until Azrael's own lips twitched up at one corner into a curious smirk. "Do you like it?"

I faltered for a response.

"I thought it might be easier if I..." he trailed off, gaze shifting as he thought through what to say. "If we didn't look so...*similar.*"

Something in my chest ached at his admission.

He'd done this...*for me?*

So, *I* would be more comfortable?

"It is," I admitted, taking in the whole picture of him. It was a minute change. They still had the same face. The same body shape. The same eyes. But it *did* make it easier somehow and I wanted to cry at the ridiculousness of it.

Tentatively, I closed the gap between us. Azrael stiffened as I hesitantly wrapped my arms around him, taking in his scent of African violets and musk, so distinctly *not* Rafe. I tensed when he wrapped his arms around me in return, but after a second, I began to relax.

"I'll kill him for what he did to you," Azrael whispered in my ear, his breath feathering over my neck, making me shudder. "And this time, I will *not* hesitate."

He kissed the top of my head and pulled back, eyes

gazing into mine, gauging something. Perhaps whether or not I believed him.

I wished I could.

But the truth was he had the opportunity to kill his brother once and he didn't take it. There was a chance he would squander it a second time. It was no matter, though. If Azrael failed a second time, *I* would succeed. I'd already decided. If an opening presented itself; I'd take him out, even if it meant I didn't walk away from the fight.

Azrael's eyes hardened and I looked away.

"It will not come to that," he said roughly, answering my thoughts.

I turned to leave, a little perturbed that he was inside of my head. He knew how much I hated that. But he caught me by the arm, halting me for another second. "We have much to do."

I nodded, tugging my arm from his grip, unable to stop the thought before it raced through my mind. *Not before I do my guys.*

Azrael's lips parted. I thought I saw hurt cross his features for a split second before his face was back to an expressionless mask.

"Tomorrow then," he acquiesced.

"Tomorrow," I agreed, striding back to the gym room door as he sped past me, following the path I'd taken from the lab, likely gone to check on Ethan.

I exhaled long and loud when I thought he was far enough away and no longer listening. The handle wrenched forward a heartbeat later, dragging me with it into the gym, nearly jerking my goddamned arm out of its socket. I grabbed my shoulder, cursing under my breath as I glared up into the icy blue eyes of Frost.

"Damnit, Frost," I gritted out, checking to make sure it hadn't actually dislocated. It hadn't and I sighed. Re-setting a shoulder had to be one of my least favorite experiences. Not because of the pain—my shattered foot had definitely taken the cake on that one—but because of the strange sensation of your bones not being where they should. It was, for lack of a better word, disgusting. Getting the shoulder back into the socket always made me want to hurl.

"Shit," he cursed, his deep, throaty voice bellowing in the cavernous space. "Rose, I didn't mean to— "

"Shut up," I said, mostly teasing now. "I'm good."

"The fuck did you do?" Blake demanded, appearing around Frost, affording me a full view of their glori-ously unclothed torsos. Lightly coated in a sheen of sweat.

It took a *lot* to make a vampire sweat, they must have been going extra hard.

I licked my lips, taking in how their gym shorts did absofuckinglutely nothing to conceal what was beneath.

"Rose, you good?" Blake asked, making my head snap up from his junk to his face, to find one dark brow quirked up, the ghost of a smirk playing at the edge of his mouth.

I swallowed, striding past Frost into the room, my body suddenly alive with energy. More energy than I'd felt in *days*. I'd spent too long just living day by day. Eat. Sleep. Beat up training dummies. Repeat.

"Great," I answered Blake, squatting to unzip my knee-high boots and toss them into a corner of the rectangular room. It was pretty massive considering. With one side laid out like a pay-by-the-month membership type joint with machinery all but useless to immortals and the other half a relatively barren space absolutely perfect for sparring.

"Rose, what the fuck are you doing?" Frost asked, shutting the door. "We thought we heard Az out there just now. Is he back?"

"Yup," I replied, dismissive. I didn't want to talk about *that* right now. I wanted to tackle the shit out of my guys, make them submit, and then fuck until dawn. *Yeah.* Great plan.

I pulled my long black hair back into a tight ponytail, rolling my shoulders back as I began to stretch out my back and neck, moving to my legs next. "Now. Who's going to spar with me?"

Blake grinned.

Frost's face hardened even more as if that were possible. I swore getting a smile from that great big oaf was damn near impossible sometimes. He ranged from angry to angrier and there wasn't much in between. "Not exactly a fair fight," he said, giving me a hard look.

I gave a one-shoulder shrug, backing slowly, maybe

a little provocatively towards the sparring area. "No," I agreed, turning the tables back on them. Sometimes I wondered if they forgot who I was. Always so concerned with protecting me they disregarded the fact I killed vampires for sport for *years* before I met them. Often more than one at a time. Sometimes many if they were young and inexperienced.

"It's not a fair fight…" I trailed off, winking. "For you."

Blake laughed, his eyes sparkling with mischief. "Is that so?" He asked, crossing his arms over his tatted chest.

I bit my lip, beckoning him with a finger curled inward. "Why don't you come and find out?"

Even I had to admit my guys were among the strongest of vampires their age I'd ever met. Hell, they were stronger than some I knew that were several times their ages.

It didn't unsettle me for a second. If anything, it made it all the more thrilling. Already, I could feel my senses sharpening into crystalline focus. My body and mind registering a real challenge in their next opponents.

When Blake darted forward, practically a blur of speed, I let my reflexes take over. Feeling more than seeing how he moved. I stepped out of his path and spun, shoving the back of his right shoulder. His balance faltered for an instant, but he regained it a heartbeat later, coming at me again. Trying to surprise me by faking to the left before grabbing for my right forearm.

I twisted out of his grip and landed a blow to his chest, making him bounce back a step, surprise registering in his eyes.

We circled one another for a moment, each looking for weak spots in the other's movements. On a whim, I withdrew my stake and tossed it to Frost. "If you aren't going to play, put that away would you?"

Much like a vampire had trouble containing their thirst—especially while on the hunt—I had trouble controlling my nature to stab first and ask questions later while sparring. I didn't want to get carried away. Not with my guys.

From the corner of my eye, I could see Frost's frown. How his muscles bulged as he crossed them over his chest.

Blake took advantage of my momentary distraction, managing to sweep my legs out from under me. I landed hard on my back with a gush of air leaving my lungs but was up before Frost could finish growling at Blake.

Before Blake had even turned around.

I climbed him like a fucking tree from the back, hooking my leg around his neck and using all my strength to curl my body inward and down, taking him to the ground with me in an epically beautiful chokehold. Glee made my lips turn up into a feral smile.

When Blake tapped a second later, a bubble of laughter tumbled from my lips.

"Somebody's feeling better," Blake mused with a half-smirk, as I loosened my leg hold on his throat. "That was a damn good hold, Rose."

He took a moment on the ground with my leg still wrapped loosely around his throat to grip my leg, pressing a kiss to my inner thigh before he stood, leaving me there on the ground with a quiver in my belly.

"Well," I said, wetting my dry throat with a swallow as I arched a brow at Frost. "Think you can take me down, big guy?"

Frost rolled his eyes.

"Come on, have a little fun for once."

When he still made no reply, I decided to sweeten the deal.

"Okay, how about this: indulge me here. Both of you come at me. If either of you can take me down..."

Pause for dramatic effect.

"I'll let you do," I ran a finger down the side of my breast, biting my lower lip, "whatever you want to me."

Blake's eyes widened a fraction before he whipped his head around to glare at Frost. "Man," he pleaded, glancing between Frost and me, bouncing a little on the balls of his feet. "Come on. We can take her."

Frost wiped a hand over his jaw, settling cut-glass eyes on me. "Fine, but don't say I didn't warn you."

Before he even finished the last word, he crossed

the space, his face a picture of calm as his body tightening, coiling like a snake going in for the kill.

Fuck yes.

Come to mama.

I jumped into the air, twisting my body over his head as he passed under me, ready with a spinning kick as he whirled, arms outstretched to make a grab for me. He dodged, making me remember just how fast he was for a guy so big.

A prickle skittering over my neck alerted me to Blake coming at me from behind and I dipped low, throwing out a leg to send him sprawling to his back this time. Frost managed to get a hand around my waist as I came up, pulling me hard against him.

Gripping his forearm, I swung my body to one side, effectively cartwheeling out of his grip.

"Damn, she's good."

"You know it," I replied, turning in time to see Frost's eyebrow draw down, confused.

I rushed him, blocking an attack with my arm as I slid through his defenses like a knife through butter, tucking into a roll and grabbing his leg as I went. I almost had him, too, but Blake lifted me from behind as easily as though he were lifting a small child. Yanking me from Frost and the ground to toss me through the air.

A ballsy move. If I didn't have the reflexes of a goddamned cat, I could have been seriously hurt. But he knew I'd kill the landing. He grinned at me as my

ELENA LAWSON

feet found the concrete floor again, arm out to steady myself.

A hiss came from my lips and I glared up at him, daring him to make another move.

"She's like a damned cat," Blake said.

But I was looking right at him and his lips...they weren't moving.

My lips parted. Was that...

Had I just read his mind?

"You're going down," I heard from behind me, but I whipped my head around a fraction of a second too late. Frost had me, arms like metal bars around my body, constructing like a serpent. Keeping my arms pressed hard to my sides. He dipped his head down to my ear, whispering hotly, "Concede?"

Mouth dry, I licked my lips, watching Blake saunter over like a panther stalking his prey. He stared appreciatively at my body, bound in the flesh of his best friend, and I was reminded of a time when he had me bound just as securely, in Shibari ropes, suspended from the ceiling of their loft in Baton Rouge.

Heat pooled between my thighs and a small moan escaped my lips as he ran a finger down my sweat-slicked belly below Frost's arms, dipping his fingers below the waistband of my leather pants to grab me by my cunt.

My hips bucked.

"We win," he said in a husky voice, their combined scents intoxicating me almost just as much as their

20

touch. All thoughts of a possible mind reading moment fled my thoughts. I could over analyze later. Right now, all I wanted, more than anything, was to feel my guys inside me.

"This time," I allowed. "I'll get you next time, you'll see."

Blake's grip on my pussy tightened and a whimper left my lips as a jolt of pleasure exploded through me. "I have no doubt," he replied, swallowing my whimper with a kiss that set my body on fire.

"Maybe we should take this to the bedroom," Frost said in a brusque whisper, nipping at the crook of my neck as Blake moved his lips down, kissing my chin. My jugular. Batting Frost's arms out of the way so he could lay another kiss on my chest. All the sensations running through me made me want to scream.

I needed them. Bad.

I couldn't wait to go back to the bedroom. This was happening here. Now. Ethan would be finished with those vials any second now. He could join us.

"I need you to fuck me," I demanded, my voice a breathy hiss. "Fuck me until I can't walk. Got it?"

"Your wish is our command," Frost growled in my ear, releasing me from his hold to unzip my shirt from the back, plucking it from my naked flesh in the blink of an eye.

"Hold her."

Frost pulled my arms up over my head obediently, as Blake knelt and jerked my leather pants off. The air in the gym was cool against my heated skin. I moaned at the sensation and Frost took that opportunity to plunge his tongue into my mouth. At the same time, Blake's tongue delved into the slickness between my legs.

My knees buckled and two strong pairs of arms caught me. Blake grabbed my thighs and hoisted me up between them, wrapping my legs around his head.

And fuck if that wasn't erotic, but it wasn't what I wanted. I wanted them inside.

Now if only I could get my brain to work long enough to tell them that. Frost tweaked a pebbled nipple between his fingertips, and I moaned into his mouth. My core tightened and flexed trying to press closer to Blake, but he pulled back, kissing the inside of my thighs.

"Fuck me, please." I arched my back, tightening my legs around his head.

Blake growled, scraping his fangs along my inner thigh. I shuddered, waiting for the pain and pleasure of his bite.

"Didn't she say we could do whatever we wanted if we won?" he asked, his dark eyes glancing over to Frost.

The smirk tugged at Frost's mouth shot a bolt of electricity through my core. "Those were the terms of the agreement."

The excitement those words brought almost pushed me over the edge. My skin crawling with the need for them, and it sounded as if they were getting ready to fuck with me rather than fuck me. Oh, there would be hell to pay later, and judging by their expressions, they were looking forward to it.

"Take her over there," Blake said, his voice rough.

Frost's grip on me tightened and Blake lowered my legs from his shoulders. I felt like a piece of meat being carried across the room. There was a large contraption in the corner with a bench and multiple handles for weight lifting. Blake didn't waste any time stripping his shorts off, and my mouth watered at the sight of him hard and ready. He settled on the bench and lowered me into his lap.

"Hold onto the bar above your head and don't let go," he growled into my shoulder.

His voice against my skin made me shudder and I did as he said. Frost adjusted the weights so I would be able to suspend myself from it without pulling the bar down. He watched with half-lidded eyes as Blake's cock slid achingly slow into me, his arms under my legs.

I didn't know how he was so good at restraining himself, but it was the most exquisite form of torture. I wanted it hard and brutal, I wanted to feel all of them, all of my guys, our puzzle of four souls. This delicate attention was more like Ethan's handiwork, which wasn't bad. It was just so unlike them.

Frost's shorts hit the floor just as Blake started moving. The combination of that delicious friction and the striptease in front of me had me panting and reinforcing my grip on the bar. Blake's nose brushed across my shoulder and I tilted my head to the side in silent permission. He chuckled and thrust harder for a few strokes, pressing light kisses across my neck.

Were they deliberately withholding their bite from me?

"So impatient," he murmured against my skin.

In front of us, Frost had his cock in his hand, stroking lightly. I wanted it, in my hand, in my mouth, in me anywhere he could fit it. He approached and knelt, and I barely had time to register what he was about to do through the haze of lust when his tongue lashed out at my sex.

I nearly lost my grip on the bar.

"Don't let go," Blake commanded.

Fuck.

Holding on was a lot harder than I'd anticipated. When my whole body wanted to go limp under their dual assault. Blake held my hips still as his thrusts picked up and Frost's tongue pressed and swirled. My head fell back onto Blake's shoulder and he groaned, teeth pressing against the tender flesh but not yet piercing.

"Do it, please," I begged.

My stomach twisted, a quickening sensation rushing through me. Frost's hands caressed my breasts and I moaned loudly, pushing Blake's restraint over the edge as his teeth sunk in, his pace coming unhinged.

His venom crashed into my building orgasm and exploded through me violently.

My head spun with the ferocity of it. Blake growled into my shoulder as he followed me over the edge. My arms were burning with the strain of holding myself up and my grip started to slip.

Fighting was one thing but holding your weight still like that was brutal.

Blake wrapped an arm around my middle, pulling my legs back to set my knees on the bench on either side of him. "You can let go now."

I almost crumpled with relief and Blake kept hold of me, pressing me against his chest so I didn't tip over.

Frost's attention latched onto a noise across the room and I was able to focus on the last piece of my puzzle coming toward us. My mouth stretched into a lazy grin as the little minx purred, anticipation coiling in the pit of my stomach.

The tips of Ethan's ears were red, but he moved steadily closer, his growing erection visible under his clothes. His gaze moved over me hungrily before he glanced at Frost for direction.

I reached for him, my arm strength returning as the blood rushed back to my fingertips. Frost moved back and I grabbed Ethan's waistband, unzipping his pants. His breath hitched as I tugged them down, freeing his cock and wrapping my hand around the silky steel.

I wanted to taste it.

But Ethan shocked me when he grabbed me by the

waist, hoisting me off of Blake's lap and pressing me to him. My legs instinctively wrapped around his waist, my arms around his neck, his length trapped between us. Our eyes met and I saw the question in them, the ever-present need for consent, for my permission.

My lips on his were my answer. I tried to communicate my desperate need, but he maintained his sweet, soft kisses even as he maneuvered to enter me. Hands and lips glided across my back, my ass, the contact lighting me on fire.

What was going on? As much as I loved this gentle side, I had a craving I wanted satisfied and my guys weren't giving it to me.

"What's wrong?" Ethan asked, noticing my distraction.

I met all of their eyes. "You're going too easy on me," I accused, mostly leveling the accusation at the two behind me. My lip curled and my voice hardened. "What I wanted was all of you in your own way. What I want is for all of us to be connected, together."

Frost trailed his fingers up my arm, chasing them with kisses. "What would make you happy, Rosie?"

Did he want me to take the lead? He hadn't given up that control since we'd reconnected, but I wasn't about to turn it down. I pulled him close and made my demands, sweetening my voice.

"I want you behind me, in my ass," I whispered against his lips. Then I turned to Blake on my other side and smirked deviously, stroking his cheek. "And I want you in his."

I wasn't sure if he'd go for that. Since we'd been back together, I hadn't seen him interact much with the other guys. I also knew his lust for dominance in the bedroom, though he was comfortable with the occasional command from Frost. His jaw clenched, but the corners of his lips tilted up and he gave a tight nod.

Holy fuck. Of all the places to not have any fucking mirrors. Maybe I should've gotten a camera. This was something I absolutely wanted to watch. Just the idea of it made me dizzy.

Adjusting his grip on my thighs, Ethan slid me slowly down his length. I bucked my hips, taking him all in one swift stroke. He hissed between his teeth and pressed his forehead to mine.

I felt fingers spreading my ass cheeks and braced for pressure, so when Frost's tongue swept across my asshole I nearly jumped off of Ethan. The sensation was both fucking incredible and jarring, if only because I hadn't been expecting it.

"What are you doing?" I squeaked, twisting to look at him.

Frost cocked an eyebrow, fighting a smile at my reaction. "I didn't bring lube to the gym."

He dipped his tongue back in and I leaned forward against Ethan's chest, muffling a moan against his skin. Frost's hand soothed across my lower back, and then there was the familiar pressure, what I'd been waiting for. He eased inside me slowly and I gasped as he inched his way to filling me up.

This was what I'd fucking wanted.

Ethan's grip tightened and I ran my fingers into his golden hair, kissing him hard, waiting for them to start moving. For something to happen. Frost swept his tongue across my shoulder where Blake had bitten me and wrapped his arms around my stomach, taking some of my weight from Ethan, but they remained still.

I glanced back over Frost's shoulder to see Blake standing behind Frost, head hanging low. I thought for a moment I'd asked too much of him, that maybe he really was uncomfortable with it. Then Frost's eyelids fluttered, and his breath hitched in his chest. He gave a short half-thrust as Blake entered him.

All the pieces were connected.

"Now fucking move," I growled.

They did just that. My voice bounced off the walls as they worked me relentlessly, finding the perfect rhythm between them. Another orgasm built up rapidly, and even though I didn't have a good view, just knowing all of them were connected in the most vulnerable way made me so fucking hot.

My moans grew louder as Frost's hands swept up my stomach to grab my breasts, flicking his thumb over my stiff nipples. His breath mixed with Ethan's on my shoulder and I threw my hair to the side. I saw their eyes meet and Frost leaned back, nodding at Ethan.

One of Frost's hands left my stomach and reached back, pulling Blake's head down to the soft flesh of his neck. I tangled my fingers in Ethan's hair and did the same.

"Bite me."

Frost bucked hard and groaned the same time Ethan's teeth found my vein. Another orgasm ripped through me, my throaty moan mingling with the mixed tones of my guys as we pushed each other off the edge together.

It was fucking glorious.

2

We slept most of the day away and honestly? I feel like I could've slept most of the night away too. With the phantom feel of my guys' hands on my body, their cocks filling me, I could have ridden the wave of delicious ecstasy and exhaustion for at least another nine hours.

But duty called.

With Rose's Sunblock finished percolating or doing whatever the fuck it needed to do before Ethan could be ready to use it, it was time to make good on our promise to the vampires in the bunker. They'd waited long enough. Travelled from all over with us on only a promise.

Giving them a taste was the least we could do and would secure their loyalty. Then we could begin planning. With the advantage of the sun, we'd be undefeatable, right?

I hoped so.

Azrael had taken the room opposite ours in this area of the bunker. Where ours seemed to have once belonged to a higher ranking official in the military, equipped with a large bed, desk, and armoire—his was converted from a massive storage room to the bedroom it was now. I knew because for the first couple of days after we got here, I kept accidentally entering his room instead of ours, my head still stuck somewhere in the clouds, detached from my body.

I paused outside of his door, not bothering to knock. He would hear me, and if he didn't, he'd have already heard my thoughts.

Can I come in? I pushed the thought inside.

The door opened a moment later, revealing Azrael, still sleep rumpled. His new shorter hair sticking up at an odd angle on one side. Shirtless. His pants hanging low on his hips, revealing the deep 'V' shape of his Adonis belt.

I cleared my throat. "Ethan is almost ready," I told him. "We can start bringing them in soon."

He searched my gaze, making a small shudder of unease run through me. What was he looking for?

"You look better," he said, completely disregarding what I told him.

"Thanks?"

A muscle in his jaw twitched and he looked away. "I'll be down in a few minutes."

"Are you okay?" I asked, feeling like an idiot as soon

as the words left my lips. He didn't strike me as the sort of man—the sort of vampire—who would like being viewed as anything less than okay. Ever.

Giving credence to my thoughts, he flinched, upper lip curling.

"I didn't mean..." I trailed off. "Never mind. I'll see you down there."

Azrael's grip on the door tightened to the point where I could've sworn I saw the metal dent beneath his fingertips as I turned away. Then I remembered.

"Wait," I said, turning back. "Last night I—well, I think I somehow accidentally read Blake's mind. Maybe Frost's, too."

"When? How did it happen?" He demanded, the gears turning behind his mismatched eyes.

I gave a small shrug. "When we were sparring. I just thought they were talking, but then their lips weren't moving and— "

Azrael nodded sharply, silencing whatever I'd been about to say next. "Good. That's very good. Let's test that later, shall we?"

"Alright. Sure."

I hadn't practiced at all since my return, but I figured managing to break Rafe's compulsion and escape his clutches in NYC meant I'd earned a well-deserved break. That break, it seemed, was now over. It was probably for the best. I would need to be sharp not just with my fighting skills, but with my mind as well if I expected to be able to hold my own in this fight.

There would be vampires who were hundreds of years older than my guys fighting alongside Rafe. And though they wouldn't be as strong as him, of body or mind, all it would take was one slip up. One moment when I wasn't completely focused and many of them would have the ability to try to compel me. They would only need to hold me for a second to end me.

But I would only need to hold them for a second to end them, too.

Azrael was right, it was time to train again, much as I didn't want to. Bring on the migraines.

Azrael's lips had pressed into a thin line and he looked over my expression before breaking eye contact and stepping back into his room.

"If you'll excuse me," he said, brows drawing together as the door swung shut, sealing him inside and me on the outside with a shudder running up my spine.

Okay then…

Was it just me or was that hella fucking awkward? I mean, I knew it was mostly me having a hard ass time differentiating between him and his twin but…I felt like there was something else there making it awkward as hell.

I shook my head, snapping my focus away from Rafe and resolving to try harder to separate my disgust for Raphael from my…whatever I felt…for Azrael.

The more I saw him and talked to him the better it

would get. Things would go back to normal between us.

I ground my teeth, walking to the lab to find Ethan, wondering exactly *what* our normal looked like.

My belly flipped at the memory of Azrael's hands on my body, pressing me into cold, unyielding stone as his lip...

Fuck.

Well, it was safe to say the idea of Azrael still turned me on. I just needed to get over my shit and—well, I didn't know what would happen then, but the possibilities made my skin alternately bristle and flush with lust and crawl with dread.

"Rose?" Ethan called from the lab, his voice carrying through the open door. "That you?"

I rounded the corner, grinning up at him as I entered, and he came to meet me at the door. He stole a quick kiss from my lips and then twined his fingers with mine, dragging me to his worktable.

Set atop it were about thirty small pots of reddish-black ink. And a bottle of pills filled with a fine powder in the same reddish black color. The transparent capsules made the contents look as though they were shimmering.

"Looks like you're ready to go," I mused, gesturing to the pill bottle. "What are those?"

He scooped up the glass bottle and considered it with the gleam of a mad scientist in his eye. It made me chuckle quietly to myself, breaking his focus. He turned to me with a lopsided grin that made my insides squeeze and my toes curl.

What the hell were these guys doing to me?

"They're the same formula as the tattoo ink," Ethan explained, unscrewing the lid to grab one of the pills out and pass it to me. "Modified slightly, dehydrated, and ground into powder."

"You think they'll have the same effect as the ink?"

His brows drew down slightly as he took the pill back from my fingers and dropped it back into the bottle with the others. "I'm not sure. They need to be tested. But yes. Maybe."

"Why do I get the feeling you're planning on testing these yourself?"

He grinned wickedly at me. "You don't think I'd give an untested product to our troops, do you?"

Darkly, I thought, *yes,* I would rather that, but I didn't say it. Instead, I just cleared my throat and licked my dry lips, distracted by the circles he was rubbing in the back of my hand with his thumb. "Don't worry," he said, reading my thoughts. "I'll be staying close to the entrance just in case."

I nodded.

"Where's Az? We need to get started if we're going to get the first batch of recruits out into the daylight before nightfall. The others will have to wait until tomorrow."

"He's— "

"Here," Az said, appearing like a ghost behind me.

I stifled a girly squeal and chided myself internally for the gut reaction.

You're the motherfucking Black Rose.

You're the motherfucking Black Rose.

Stop being a goddamned baby.

The corner of Az's lips twitched, and I groaned internally.

Get out of my head!

His attention turned to Ethan. "Ready?"

Ethan gave a short nod, beginning to gather the ink pots into the bag containing his tattooing equipment. He slipped the pills into the side pocket and Azrael glanced at them curiously, though he didn't ask aloud what they were or what they were intended for. All of that information, I assumed, he's just gleaned from Ethan's mind.

"Blake and Frost are on their way. They'll accompany us. We'll need to meet the sun with the recruits to ensure none go outside the protection of the warding ring."

My brows furrowed. "I'm coming too," I said, hating how the words came out edged in a question instead of the statement I intended.

Azrael frowned.

"You've killed literal hundreds of our kind, Rose." It was Ethan who spoke. "For all we know, you could be responsible for the deaths of some of the recruits' friends. Families. It may not be safe."

"Hold up," I stopped him, feeling the heat of anger

swell beneath my breastbone. "Wasn't it you who said they would come around? Once they saw I could give them the sun that they would, like, worship me?"

"How do you expect them to fight alongside me in battle to come if you won't even let them near me."

Azrael and Ethan shared a look, clearly, I was missing something.

I didn't fucking like it.

"You haven't given them the sun yet, Rose," Az said finally.

"Well, they better start getting used to me," I said, crossing my arms over my chest. "You can read their minds. You'll be able to anticipate any sort of attack and I'll be more than happy to dispose of any who try."

More than happy.

"Very well," Azrael said after a pause. "But you will remain by my side. Can you do that?"

"Fine," I all but growled.

I hadn't been outside in *days*. I didn't know how vampires survived it. If I didn't see the sun, or hell, at least *the sky* soon I was going to go mental down here. Besides, they really did need to get used to me. If I was the one who was to lead them alongside Azrael.

"What's going on?" Frost asked, his growl reverberating from the down the hall before he and Blake stepped into the lab. "You're letting her come?"

Letting me?

These guys were forgetting who I was.

Nobody *let* me do anything. I did what I damn well pleased.

"Is that problem?" I couldn't keep the ire from my voice as I levelled a murderous stare on Frost.

"They've been on rations since we arrived," Blake said. "A small amount of blood from a blood bag given each day at the edge of dawn. They're all hungry."

"If they can't control themselves, then they can't be trusted around other humans. If they can't be trusted around other humans, then *I don't want them.*"

Ethan sighed. "We don't really have the luxury of picking and choosing— "

"Can we just," I blurted, shoulders tense. "*Not* do this. In a matter of months—*weeks really*—I've gone from vampire assassin to spearheading an army of them. I just..." I trailed off. "I need to see *who* it is I'm fighting with. 'Kay?"

I left before any of them could reply, storming down the hall with purposeful strides.

I'd do what I needed to to take out Rafe and his army once and for all. To usher in a new era of vampire. With new laws. That was my ultimate plan after all, wasn't it?

To make the streets safer for humans. Taking out Rafe would do most of the job, but then the rest of the vampire population would need to be policed. Culled. Given a strict set of rules to live by. No torturing. No killing.

It was going to be either blood bags or *humane* feeding. Capture, compel, feed, release. No non-consensual touching. No keeping humans as blood bags for a midnight snack.

They would fall in line or die.

Azrael caught up to me a second later, and I didn't need to turn my head to see the look he was giving me from the corner of my eye. He was watching me curiously. Warily. I had no doubt he'd just read all my thoughts. He knew what I was hoping to accomplish if we survived the fight.

To create a world where humans and vampires could co-exist. Where my job of slaughtering them on a daily basis was no longer necessary, or at least, where it was only necessary when someone broke the rules.

I couldn't give up the hunt any more than a human being could give up water or oxygen. It was in my blood. The need to kill. To dole out justice. Revenge was written in the fine print of my blood, and no matter how much they took from me, it would never fade.

"Bring the first group into the antechamber," Azrael barked to the guys, leading us up a flight of stairs and through a coded door. Into the wide space where we first entered. The heavy steel garage-type door on the far wall was the last barrier between us and the sunlight.

Blake, Ethan, and Frost forked off from Az and me, going to the door opposite the one we entered from. The one leading to the main barracks. Ethan tossed his tattoo bag to Azrael and then they vanished through to the other side.

My heart gave a sharp little twist that they were in there without me. Just in case anything was to happen.

But if I expected them to trust I was capable of defending myself, then I supposed it was only fair I trusted them, too. They were strong. Smart. They'd be fine.

Even if there were nearly two hundred vampires on the other side of that door.

Azrael made his way casually to the wall where a folding table was leaning and lifted it with a flick of his wrist, smoothly setting it up in what appeared to be a single fluid motion.

Christ, the guy even made menial tasks look good.

His mismatched gaze flicked up to meet mine for an instant before he went back to the wall to grab two chairs, creating a sort of sad-looking bistro table.

It would have to do.

Once he was finished, he came to stand next to me, a placid expression on his face. I resisted my instinct to look away from him. To ignore his presence. To super-impose the image of Rafe's insanity onto his features.

Instead, I looked at him. Really looked. Noting the subtle differences, I'd noticed once before. How he didn't have his eyes almost perpetually squinted as Rafe did. How his jaw seemed stronger, more filled out. And his brothers seemed more gaunt.

And his hair, though I was still getting used to it,

really did create a massive divide between him and his twin. Honestly? It was hot.

I mean, the long hair was hot, too. But now...

My inner lioness roared back to life and I shivered involuntarily, pleased that I'd been able to defeat my mind and see Azrael. *Just Azrael.* If only for a moment.

"Rose, if you don't stop thinking like that, I'm going to fuck you right here against this wall until you shake. Is that clear?"

I gasped a little, cursing myself for how my sex instantly wetted at the thought. Screamed internally.

The door opposite us opened and I schooled my features, praying the furious heat in my cheeks wasn't super visible where Az and I stood near the shadowy wall.

Thank fuck they were back though because I wasn't entirely sure I wouldn't have allowed Azrael to keep that threat.

Frost and Ethan led the group and Ethan brought up the rear. I counted thirty-seven of them.

"Rose!" A semi-familiar voice called, and I squinted into the throng, finding her face.

Valentina waved from amid a group of what looked like about eight males who hadn't moved more than several feet away from her, even though the rest of the grouping seemed to be fanning out.

I was so distracted checking them all out I didn't register the attack until it was already in motion.

The vamp darted forward, his eyes open wide and

crazed with bloodlust. His hands outstretched like claws. The vein in his neck popping.

Azrael was quick to intercede, but I wanted this one.

He didn't see me coming. I elbowed the ancient vamp in the side, surprising him just enough so he sidestepped the five inches I needed to soar past, raise my stake, and strike.

The blood-crazed vamp feinted to one side, but I didn't let him get far, a wicked smile coming over my face. "Oh no you don't," I said, my voice light. Playful.

I caught him by his long ponytail and threw him to the floor, using his own momentum against him when he tried to whirl on me. My stake was plunged five inches into muscle and sinew before he knew what hit him. I felt his body twitch beneath me as I straddled him, the life going out of his eyes.

I vaguely registered I probably looked like a psychopath, grinning as I was; but I didn't care. In fact, I could use it to my advantage.

With a glare around at all the vampires around us, their stares alternately afraid, disgusted, angry, and uncaring as I stood. "Anyone else having a little trouble controlling their thirst?" I shouted, my voice echoing. Arms stretched wide.

"Anyone?" I repeated, catching Ethan and Blake fist-bumping by the makeshift Tattoo table, and Frost grinning with his arms crossed over his chest. Azrael, however, did *not* seem to be enjoying this.

He glared at the grouping of vampires, and I knew in my bones he was almost *hoping* one of them would try to move in for the kill. Just as I had been.

When none moved so much as an inch, I withdrew my stake from the vampire's chest and wiped it unceremoniously on his dark blue t-shirt, sheathing it back in its holster on my thigh. "Good," I said, a little disappointed if I was being honest.

"You probably already guessed this, but I'm Rose."

"The Black Rose…" someone whispered, though I didn't see who.

"That's right," I agreed. "The one and only."

Azrael gave me a cursory glance before gesturing to where Ethan had begun setting up his things on the table. "You will form a line," he roared, and even though the compulsion was not directed at me, I could feel it in the air like a phantom weight and cringed.

The vampires moved into a curving line from the table all the way to the wall, hugging the wall to the door. "You will *not* step out of this line until it is your turn to receive your dose. You will then sit until Ethan is finished with you and resume your place in the line until it is time to go outside, at which point you will not move until given further instruction."

"Az—" I started, but he cut me off with a look.

This wasn't how we were supposed to do this. Rafe's army was controlled. Compelled. Our army was meant to follow us of their own free will's.

Not like this, I directed the thought at him, glancing

furtively at Valentina and her guys, uncomfortable under the weight of his compulsion. *Not like this.*

"I can't take any chances."

I stared at him long and hard, watching his jaw tighten. And then some more before he finally inhaled, lifting his chin a fraction of an inch before the compulsion I could feel in the atmosphere dissipated and the vampires collectively released a breath.

"We are not like Raphael," I said, letting my voice be heard by all. "You all have a choice here."

"But I suggest," I added, letting some venom into the words. "You choose *very* wisely."

None moved out of the line. None even spoke as the first vampire took the seat opposite Ethan and he guided his arm onto the table. He didn't ask what the vampire would like tattooed, he just began inking the blood-tainted ink into his flesh. Working quickly, I could already make out the beginnings of the outline of a reddish black rose coming into form on the vampire's forearm.

3

"*A*re you sure this is going to work?" Valentina whispered to me, managing to extricate herself from her harem for a moment. "I mean, I don't doubt Ethan, it's just— "

"You don't want to be fried to a crisp?"

"Yeah. That."

"I've seen it work," I reassured her, trying to ease some of the leftover tension out of my shoulders. Though Azrael ordered the body of the vamp I'd staked be cleared away and the blood mopped up, there was still a red stain as a reminder that at any time any of the other vampires could try to take me out. Whether from hunger or rage at who I was.

"You'll be alright," I added, moving to pat her on the shoulder but she shifted so quickly out of the way I only wound up patting air. I cocked my head at her.

"No o-offence," she said with a little stutter. "I'm

doing alright but I'm still a newborn. And *um...*" she trailed off, furtively glancing at me from beneath her lashes. "You smell, like, really good."

I stifled a laugh. "Fair enough."

With a tight smile, she returned to her group of males, one of which I noticed slid his hand into her back pocket.

"What about you?" I overheard Frost ask and returned to the table with Azrael on my heels. He wasn't kidding about sticking close to me. Frost and Blake had just finished receiving their own tattoos. For Blake, a dove, and for Frost a geometric wolf I had to admit looked pretty bad ass even though it was rather small against the width of his forearm.

Ethan set down his things and dug out the bottle of pills. "I wanted to test these," he said, giving the bottle a rattle.

My lips pursed.

"If they work, it'll be a lot easier than tattooing our entire army a second time when they're ready to fight."

"Man," Blake said, grabbing the bottle to check out the pills himself. "Why didn't you tell us? This is awesome."

"I didn't want to say anything until I knew whether they would work."

"I have every confidence they will," Azrael agreed. "In fact, I'll take one as well."

Ethan stared a little agape at Azrael, floundering for

a response. "I'd really rather test them myself first. Just in case—I mean, it's possible they could— "

Azrael snatched up the pill bottle from Blake and had a pill out of the jar and into his mouth less than a second later. He then held the open jar out to Ethan, one brow raised.

Ethan considered Az for a moment, maybe checking for signs of poisoning. Making sure the other vampire wasn't going to spontaneously combust. I watched too, guiltily feeling a little glad Azrael took the first one.

Though still horrified something could happen to him all the same.

Fucking idiots, the both of them.

They should have tested it on one of the recruits first.

I shuddered at how easily that thought came but it was the truth. It was what I would rather. And if that made me a selfish bitch then so be it.

After what felt like the longest minute ever, Ethan took the outstretched bottle and lid, dry swallowing one of his own pills with a grimace. "I'll need to do something about the capsules," he said with a sour face.

"It tasted like shit," Azrael agreed.

To which everyone gave a short laugh.

"Did you just…" I began incredulously, squinting up at Azrael. "Did you just *curse*."

"*Shit* is hardly a curse word," he argued, but I noted

how he looked almost stricken for an instant before he said it.

"It's kind of a curse word, man," Ethan teased.

"Clearly I spend too much time in your heads," Azrael said, erasing all smiles and every last trace of laughter with his words.

With a triumphant gleam in his eyes, he took a long swallow of air and brought his hands together. "Shall we go out for a stroll?"

Frost cleared his throat and spun, hollering at the gathering of vampires. "Everyone stay close. We've only given a small dosage of the elixir to each of you and you'll want to be in close proximity to shelter for when it wears off."

Not exactly a threat, but an effective way of putting it.

Try to leave and you'll die.

Stay and you might get another taste someday.

One vampire in particular looked as though he was on his way to the most important moment of his life. Like a wedding or the birth of a child. He was old, I could tell by my vampy-sense. He likely hadn't seen the sun in at least a hundred years if not more. If I wasn't mistaken, it looked like there might have been the beginnings of tears in his eyes.

Frost went forward to open the door and the vampires collectively backed up. Their fear outweighing their excitement. Only my guys holding their ground near the door kept them from fleeing entirely.

The hinges creaked as it was raised, slowly at first, but then it was like Frost decided to say fuck it because he wrenched the thing the rest of the way up, letting a deluge of orange-hued light into the chamber. The warmth against my cheeks made me shudder with delight even though the air temp outside was somewhere that had to be near freezing even though there was yet to be snow on the ground.

I watched Az and Ethan carefully as the sun hit them, noting how Ethan's skin reddened on his cheeks and how he grimaced. I was about to pummel him back into the shadows when I saw how that redness was already beginning to fade.

My eyes widened. "It worked?" I asked, unable to hide the surprise from my voice.

"You really have that little confidence in me?" Ethan asked and I punched him in the arm before pulling him into an embrace.

"You are incredible, you know that?"

My heart swelled as he wrapped his arms around my middle, nuzzling his face into the crook of my neck. "Not nearly as incredible as you. You gave us the sun. We could never give you anything nearly as meaningful."

"You already have," I whispered back, going on tip toe to plant a kiss on his lips before stepping away to examine how the others were holding up.

Azrael looked alright if a little stiff. Much like the first time I saw him meet the sun, he stood strictly still, though this time, he did not shed a tear. He simply looked straight on into the blazing ball of light slowly descending down toward the horizon in the distance. "It really is beautiful," he muttered so quietly I almost hadn't heard him. "I'd forgotten…"

My heart gave a sharp pang in my chest and reflexively, I took his hand, shocking him out of his reverie enough that his body jolted slightly, and he had to blink several times to reorient himself. Then his hand closed over mine and he brought it up to his lips for a chaste kiss that made my insides twist.

"Thank you," he said quietly, dragging his gaze from the horizon to my face for an instant before he regarded the others.

They all trudged forward, slowly at first, and then with increasing speed as one after the other entered into the direct light and didn't burn. Laughter filled the chamber, booming out into the last dregs of the day.

Some ran right out into the gravel lot of the entryway, jumping high into the air as though they could reach out and touch the sky. Others, much like Azrael, just stared. Speechless. Tears-eyed. In revert awe.

One sobbed openly.

My hand around Azrael's tightened as I realized just how unprepared I was for this. Their emotions…they were so *human*. So pure.

"Thank you," one vampire woman said, inclining

her head to me and then dropping onto one knee. *"Thank you."*

Another dropped to his knee beside her. "Nothing can ever repay a gift of this magnitude," the one who had been sobbing said through stuttering breath. "But you will have me at your side for as long as you wish."

I gaped up at Azrael, a little disconcerted.

This, also, had *not* been expected.

Several others were tipping their heads in agreement all around.

"We're with you," one muttered.

"Until death," another agreed.

"Told you guys she was fucking *awesome*," Valentina shouted, shoving one of her blood mates.

A strangled grunt from my side brought my attention back to Azrael though. He flinched, releasing my hand to bring a hand up to his face.

The whites of his eyes were turning red, and there was a slow-growing patch of flesh beneath that was turning from red to *fucking black* really goddamned fast.

Growing and spreading like a fast-moving plague, within an instant it covered the entire right half of his face and was quickly moving down his neck. Worse, he seemed almost paralyzed from it.

I flew into motion like a bat out of hell, tearing the nearest vampire's shirt directly from their back to cover Azrael's face and then practically body checking him into the shadows. My heart like a war drum in my ears.

"Ethan!" I shouted behind me. "Ethan *get out of the sun!*"

Frost damn near tore Ethan's arm out of its socket, grabbing him and shoving him back without question at my command.

Ethan whirled, finding my panicked eyes among all the whispering, now nervous vampires surrounding us. He managed to get out of Frost's grasp. "No. Wait. I need to see how long it lasts. I need the data."

"Like hell," Blake argued, planting a hand on Ethan's other arm, but Ethan kicked Blake's legs out from under him and glared at Frost.

"I need to do this. I'll move as soon as I have to."

"It happened fast," I hollered back, out of breath more from panic than any sort of exertion. I felt Azrael struggle beneath me and released him, letting him tear the shirt from his scorched face.

Oh my god.

Holy shit it wasn't healing.

Why wasn't it healing.

"Eth!" I called again, ready to abandon Az to go drag him over here too.

This time when Ethan saw Azrael's face, he paused, mouth going agape.

"That's enough experimenting for one day," Frost growled at his friend. "*Move* or I'll move you."

Ethan nodded, his fists clenching, and I loosed a relieved sigh.

Until his eyes widened, and his head tipped back in a cry of anguish. His body buckling as he fell to his knees.

Though he didn't quite make it that far. Frost had him by the shoulders and tossed him across the room. He *cracked* against the wall and slumped to the ground, rolling onto his stomach with his hands up as though wanting to touch something on the back of his neck but not able to.

I didn't realize I was shaking until Azrael gave my arm a tight squeeze. "*Go,*" he gritted out with the half of his mouth that wasn't black char. "Go to him. I'm fine. I think it's healing."

It sure as fuck didn't look like it, but I did as he said, needing to check if Ethan was okay. I rushed to him as the vampires slowly flooded back inside, creeping back towards the shadows but not yet leaving the sunlight.

Distantly, heard Valentina explaining to them how Azrael and Ethan had taken pills. A new trial. And how it clearly hadn't worked.

I reached Ethan a second later, hands fluttering over the mess of cracked black skin over the back of his neck. "Oh shit. *Oh shit.*"

"What does it mean?" I thought I heard him say between grunts, his voice strained and breathy. He muttered something else about a formula and a lot of big words I didn't understand. Blake and Frost were there too, appearing at my sides before I could blink.

"I'll get him inside," I said, carefully dragging Ethan's arm over my shoulders. "Frost, you get Azrael. Blake, can you get everyone else back to their barracks?"

Blake nodded.

"Rosie," Frost began, his voice strained as he looked between Azrael just now getting unsteadily to his feet, and Ethan, who was shaking as I helped him to stand.

"Just do it," I barked, unable to maintain calm. Unable to be patient. My blood pumping too violently to be gentle. Now would be the perfect moment to take out one of the oldest vampires in the entire world. He was clearly weak. Weaker than I'd ever seen him and that scared the absolute fucking shit out of me.

Any one of the thirty-seven vamps here could try something. We couldn't risk that.

"Do it now," I reinforced, jabbing the code into the door leading back to our wing of the bunker.

"Rose," Ethan croaked, unable to finish the sentence, his head hanging against his chest.

I patted his ribs where I held him. "You're going to be okay," I told him staunchly, because I didn't know what the hell I'd do if he wasn't.

4

*E*than moaned as I lowered his body to the bed. His hands fisted in the rumpled sheets as he buried his face into a pillow, breathing heavily.

My hand raised to stifle a sound of horror from fleeing my lips. I didn't want him to worry.

"Is it...bad?" He asked.

I considered the charred black flesh covering the back of his neck, stomach roiling. "No," I lied. "It's alright. It's going to heal. We just have to wait."

"You telling me that," he choked off, coughing. "Or yourself?"

I didn't answer. Couldn't.

Instead, I sat beside him, careful not to jostle the bed and pulled his stiff hand from the sheets to trap it in mine.

"Fuck," he ground out. "It feels like it burned all the way to my vocal cords."

I didn't say as much, but it sounded like it, too. His voice was scratchy and broken. Like he swallowed a bucket of razor blades instead of a drop of sunlight.

"You should have listened," I spat, unable to help myself. "I told you to get out of the sun."

"*Rose,*" It was Frost's voice that stalled me in my scolding of Ethan, and I found him walking into the room with Azrael at his side. The ancient vampire still looked unsteady and the strain around his eyes made it abundantly clear he was in agony, but he'd clearly refused Frost's aid.

Even though the char coating his face wasn't even remotely healed yet.

"What is this?" Azrael growled through gritted teeth, directing the question to Ethan, his voice just as garbled and raspy.

"I-I don't know," Ethan said, wincing as he tried to turn his head to one side to meet Azrael's gaze. "It protected us from the sun at first but then…" he trailed off.

"Then it rapidly increased the sun's potency when it wore off."

"Yes. But I don't know why. I'll need to…to do more testing."

"Like hell," Frost and I said at the exact same time.

Azrael moved to take another step into the room and nearly stumbled. I left Ethan, safely laying on the bed, and took Azrael by the arm, giving him my most poisonous glare when he tried to resist my help.

"Sit down before you fall down," I chastised him, forcing him to a seat on the edge of the bed where Ethan was laying.

Grimacing, he did as I asked.

"Generally, I am not one to stand in the way of scientific discovery, especially one as important as this..." he said, shuddering from the pain. "But I'm inclined to agree with them on this. You can't give sunlight to vampires if you turn yourself ash."

I sighed. At least *someone* was seeing sense today.

"Alright, that's enough of that," I muttered, drawing my stake, and pressing the point of it hard into my forearm. It pierced my flesh easily and a well of crimson formed, dripping down to my palm as I moved to feed Ethan what he needed to heal.

What I *hoped* would allow them to heal.

I wasn't so sure about that anymore though. I mean, my blood was in those pill capsules and look at them now.

"Azrael first," Ethan said, halting me in my tracks.

I rolled my eyes, lowering my wrist to Eth.

"Azrael. First."

"Stubborn fucker," I hissed, but turned back, doing as he asked.

Azrael regarded me and the slow closing wound on my forearm, something in his face twisting.

"Perhaps a blood bag," he said, gaze flitting to Frost and all at once the image of a similar set of fangs defiling my body came unbidden to my thoughts.

Rafe's fangs.

How they nearly made me lose myself.

How the potency of the venom had *almost* taken what little sanity I had left.

But this was *not* Rafe.

His eyes widened slightly.

I trust you.

Frost just crossed his arms and waited muttering how he wasn't going to leave two injured and *unhinged* vampires alone with me.

Azrael took my proffered arm, his deft fingers curling around my wrist and just below the crook of my elbow, sharply drawing me near, his hunger set free.

My lips parted, body clenching as he settled his fangs over the wound and bit down in one quick motion. The stab of pain ebbed so quickly I barely registered it, my body a conductor of pure unfiltered desire. His being pulsed through me like a tsunami, claiming every bone. Every nerve.

Taking *everything*.

I moaned loudly, my thighs pressing together as a fuzziness clouded my mind.

A low growl behind me reminded me Frost was there, and I did my best to tamper the desirous emotions coursing through me like a raging fire in my veins.

I wanted to touch him.

Fuck I wanted to touch him so bad.

My hands twitched, aching to feel the caress of Azrael's polished ivory skin beneath my fingertips. To feel his hard length wrapped tightly in my fist.

His hands on my arm tightened, bordering on painful and it was all I could do to stay standing there and not climb him like a wild animal.

A second later, as his fangs slid from my arm, the world came back into growing clarity and I registered how fucking *wet* my panties were. How my body was shaking.

Not from the bloodlust, but with something closer to withdrawal.

Azrael's shining eyes met mine for an instant, and in them I saw the depths of my desire mirrors back to me in brutal vividity. So clearly it made my mouth fall agape.

"Rose," Frost's gruff tone pulled me out of the trance-like state I was in and I realized what I was looking at. Around the edges of the char coating half of Azrael's face, fresh pink skin began to creep back.

It was working.

Elated, I crawled over the bed past Azrael and pushed my palm against Ethan's lips. With the angle, he wouldn't be able to reach my forearm and I didn't want him to have to move. "Bite," I ordered, shuddering as he did.

A strangled whimper left my lips, my pussy throbbing as he fed from me. I knew this wasn't the time, but I'd have given just about anything to have another good hard fucking right now. Even with the feel and memory of my guys inside of me still fresh.

My appetite for them would *never* be sated.

Not for the rest of my mortal life.

As Ethan's fangs left the muscle of my palm, a sobering thought came over me and my brows pinched, drawing down as I caught my breath after all the heavy breathing I'd just done.

...the rest of my *mortal* life...

Unlike my guys, if we survived this war, I didn't have forever.

Eventually, I would grow old.

Eventually, they wouldn't want me anymore.

Eventually, I would lose them.

And they would lose me.

It was always how it was going to end up, but I wasn't sure I'd ever truly considered it until right then. My mouth was painfully dry, and I concealed my sudden discomfort by getting unsteadily to my feet, satisfied when I saw Ethan had begun to heal, too.

"I-I need some water," I said, rushing from the bedroom to the ensuite bath, but instead of getting a drink, I went directly to the shower and turned the faucet to icy cold, tearing my clothes off and stepping inside.

I let the frigid water do its work to cool my lust-warmed flesh and to erase the invading thoughts from my mind.

We didn't have to worry about our forever. Not now.

Not yet.

5

---

*T*he mirror-like surface of the blade reflected back to me a glance of my own amber eyes as I passed it over the stone. My katana had been damaged in the fight in Baton Rouge and I hadn't had a chance to get her back up to snuff yet.

"Almost there Stabitha," I crooned to my baby. "Just a little more"

A bark of a laugh made me pause and blinked, raising my head to find three pairs of eyes watching me. I'd almost forgotten they were there.

Ethan was jotting down something in a notebook on the bed. Blake was watching something on his phone. And Frost had been doing pull ups on the metal beam running across the middle of the ceiling of our shared bedroom.

It was a rare moment of quiet where we were all

together, though no one felt the need to speak. It was an easy silence. Comfortable.

So comfortable that apparently, I felt at ease enough to mutter sweet nothings to my baby.

"What?" I asked, "You've never named your weapons?"

Frost dropped from the ceiling with a thud, one white, blond brow raising. "Stabitha?"

"For real?" Blake added, tugging a bud from his ear.

Ethan only grinned to himself, continuing to write whatever formula he'd been working through. He was still healing. It was one of the reasons none of us were off doing anything else. Instead opting to remain here with him until he was fully healed.

It had been a full day already and we'd just woken up about an hour ago and yet Ethan still had tender pink flesh pockmarked with bits of char on the back of his neck and a tiny bit on his hands. No vampire took that long to heal from a burn, even if it was the sun that'd done it.

It took every ounce of self-control I had not to flush that bottle of pills down the toilet and compel Ethan never to take another again. But I wouldn't be that person. I wouldn't ever take away their free will.

"Yes, for real," I answered unapologetically. "This is Stabitha," I repeated back to them, holding up my girl.

"And these," I added, setting her down in favor of my two favorite metal stakes. "Are Slashley and Slayla."

Ethan's lips pressed hard together, concealing a

laugh that Blake didn't mind letting free. Frost too looked like he might actually smile.

"Say what you like. All the best weapons have names. Heartsbane. Excalibur. Sting."

"But you named yours Stabitha, Slashley, and...Slay-la?" Blake asked through his laughter.

"He's right," Ethan agreed, a pained expression on his face. "Those names don't exactly inspire the same emotions as something like *Heartsbane*."

I rolled my eyes.

"Maybe not, but they've killed more vampires than any immortalized blade I'm aware of," I bit back. I lowered my voice to a whisper for dramatic effect, crooning to my babies. "Don't listen to them, they know not what they say."

Ethan laughed again, not holding it back this time. "I think the better question here is; you like fantasy?"

I cocked my head at him. "Did we or did we not watch the entire Lord of the Rings series together like eighteen times as kids?"

Ethan's steeped-tea eyes grew faraway as though he was remembering something. He smiled. "Don't know how I'd forgotten."

"Me neither," I teased. "Pretty sure I still know the whole thing word for word."

"Nerds," Blake muttered.

"You love us," I teased, to which Blake inclined his head, neither agreeing nor disagreeing.

Something tightened in my chest.

Silence fell and I resumed work sharpening my Katana for a few more minutes until Ethan heaved a sigh and snapped his journal shut, eyes hard.

He tossed it on the bed in favor of his phone and thumbed through the screens. "Hungry?" He asked me and I gave a little shrug.

"I could eat."

"You can always eat," Frost countered.

"True."

"How about Italian?"

"Do they have any Indian food? I'd kill for a good curry."

Ethan flicked over the options on the takeout app, skimming until he found what he was looking for. "Yep. You do realize its breakfast though, right?"

I finished wiping the polish from the blade and slid her back into her sheath. "Technically it's not *any* meal-time. Given we have a nighttime schedule and it's..." I tilted my phone toward me, checking the time. "Nearly eleven."

Ethan's lips twitched as he put in the order for me. The options were fairly limited around the military bunker. Not very many places delivered this far outside the nearest town. But since Azrael forbade us from leaving and I was sick to death of the reconstituted meal packets that were in the storage closet, this was the best option.

I compelled the food delivery guys to forget where they were and what or whom they say when they delivered the food so there was very little risk. It took a bit to convince Azrael, but since he allowed it once we assumed it was alright to order in three meals a night, provided there was something open to deliver it.

"Is Az still in his room?" I asked, posing the question to Frost since he was the only one who left since we brought Ethan back to the room.

Frost's eyes narrowed. "Think so. Why?"

"No reason."

That wasn't exactly true. I'd been debating on going to check on him for the last few hours since he'd left, stiff-backed and lurching to go and *rest* back in his quarters. Part of me needed to see he was alright. Another part didn't want to be alone with him.

For more than one reason...

Fear of him being the least of the two. Seeing him almost burned to a crisp in the sun had made me realize the terrifying depth of my feelings for him. He wasn't his brother.

In looks, maybe. But in every other way...

He was Azrael.

My Azrael.

My captor. My champion. My protector.

"Do you think..." Ethan trailed off, setting down his phone and pulling his bottom lip between his teeth. "Do you think you'll ever tell us what happened in New York?"

I stiffened.

"I-I'm not trying to push you—none of us are—but

we want to know so that…" he stopped short, as though he thought better of what he had been going to say.

"So that we can understand," Frost finished in a voice that was an octave short of a snarl.

"Let it go," Blake snapped at the other two, his hackles rising. "If she doesn't want to fucking talk about it then she shouldn't have to. Fucking dickheads."

Steeling myself, I folded my body into the worn lazy-boy next to the bed, biting the inside of my cheek. "No. They're right. If it were one of you, I'd want to know, too."

"But you wouldn't push us," Blake hissed, his dark eyes meeting mine. An understanding passed between us and I was brought back to that night in his room in Baton Rouge. Where he told me what his father had done to him as a child. Right beneath all of our noses. He didn't have to tell me. I didn't force him. I didn't so much as press an inch to make him.

I waited until he was ready. For him to decide.

"You're right," I agreed. "I wouldn't. But I'm getting over it. Honestly, it's not even that bad."

My stomach soured at the half truth. Part of me wanted to believe it wasn't that bad. Wondered if they would judge my weakness. After all, Rafe hadn't raped me, he only touched me. Fed from me.

And what he forced me to endure in that tiny black box wasn't anything I hadn't endured already. Right.

All at once the walls of the room where we were,

and the several feet of earth casing us in on all sides of the bunker felt too heavy. I cringed, hunching my body inward against the feeling of a tight space closing in.

It'd taken a full day for me to convince myself I *could* breathe just fine here. It was hard at first. Like the air was twice as thick. Heavy.

I took three deep lungsful of breath through my nose and blew them out between my lips.

"Rose, you don't have to— "

"It's not that," I muttered between breaths.

"It's her claustrophobia," Frost said, with an *obvious* edge to the words.

"No doubt brought on by her *stress* because we just made her think about New York," Ethan bit back.

I groaned, pinching the bridge of my nose. "I'm *fine.* Do you want me to tell you what happened or not?"

They all shut up.

I started at the beginning. How I'd tried to make a break for it the moment I'd seen him. How the reinforced glass had stopped me. I explained how he kept *wives* and intended to make me one of them.

When I got to the ugly bits, I didn't gloss over anything even though my gut reaction was to veil all of it in an aloof attitude and leave out the more gruesome details. Instead, by the time I got to the box and the memory he forced me into while I was trapped inside it, tears were in my eyes, betraying my attempt to make it sound less awful than it really was.

"And then Ethan plucked me out of the air before I could hit pavement. He saved my life."

Ethan nodded, glancing away when I looked at him to conceal the glimmer of water in his eyes.

"He…" Frost stammered, a vein popping in his forehead. His neck thick with strained muscle and teeth bared. Face red. *"He fucking…"*

He couldn't finish, fists clenching.

"I'm going to feed him his own castrated balls," Blake said plainly, his voice a dead monotone.

His pained black eyes met mine. "And then I'll hold him down while you carve him into a thousand tiny pieces."

My lips twitched. I nodded.

"I'd settle for beheading the fucker."

"Not good enough," Blake argued. "Not *nearly* good enough."

"It makes sense now," Ethan added after Frost rose to pace the room, the muscles in his face twitching as he stewed over every detail of what I told him. I'd have told him to calm down, but I knew that would do no good. It would only stoke the fire.

Best to let him get it out. As long as he didn't bring the bunker down on top of us.

"Hmm?" I said, turning my attention to Ethan, struggling to remember what he'd just said. My mind still stuck back in that penthouse suite in New York City.

Back with Penny and Luz and Yvette and the others.

Where were they now?

Were they still alive?

Has Rafe realized yet that Luz wasn't pregnant? That she never would be? Had he killed her yet?

My chest ached at the thought.

"It makes sense," Ethan repeated. "Your reaction to Azrael. I get it now. I saw something pass between you when you first saw him. He hasn't been the same since he walked out the door of that condo building in NYC. Just like you haven't been the same since you escaped."

My lips pursed. "I told him," I admitted. "I don't know why. I think in some way seeing Azrael's face— the mirror image of his brother's—I wanted to punish him. I wanted to cause him pain. I think I knew telling him would hurt.

I also just needed someone to know why I was so broken. I let him see everything that happened through my mind. I may have also told him to go, and that I couldn't stand to look at his face. Honestly, it's all a blur."

"But you *aren't* afraid of Az," Ethan hedged. "You don't hate him. You...*like him*, don't you?"

The atmosphere in the room shifted with Ethan's question. The tension thickening, making it a little bit harder to breathe again. Frost stopped pacing, spinning to capture my reaction to the question. There was no

ELENA LAWSON

mistaking how perturbed he was. Brows lowered and shoulders square.

Blake didn't seem nearly as upset by the question, however. He just regarded me with a cool ease, patiently awaiting my response.

I swallowed past the lump in my throat, trying to think of how best to explain. *If* I even should explain. If I should lie.

I shook my head, muttering to myself. "*Fuck.*"

"*Fuck,*" Frost echoed.

That single word telling them all they needed to know.

Blake stood and jabbed Frost in the ribs with his elbow, giving him a stern look before coming to sit opposite me on the edge of the bed near Ethan.

"You could have a harem of hundreds if you chose to," he said, no trace of anger in his voice or in his eyes. He was being sincere.

"I'm not a vampire," I reminded him. "I don't *do* harems."

He laughed at that, swiping an arm wide gesturing to Ethan and Frost. "Actually, you kind of do."

"And aside from drinking blood and immortality, you're the closest it gets to a modern-day vampire. Some might argue that you are the most authentic vampire there is, seeing as you're the last living Vocari."

He had a point there.

"I can only speak for myself," Ethan added a moment later. "But if you have feelings for Azrael, I

74

don't think you should fight them. At least...not on our account."

"*Eth*," Frost hissed, looking like he might just cross the room and pummel him through the mattress.

"He's right, Frost," Blake said, standing again, his body braced to fend off Frost's attack, should the larger vamp try anything.

He wouldn't, though. No matter how angry. Ethan was still healing.

Blake on the other hand, well that was his choice if he wanted to go toe to toe when Frost was this pissed off. They wouldn't kill each other, but I wouldn't be licking their wounds for them later, either.

"You know he's right. Every male vampire in this bunker wants her as their blood mate now. And she could have them all on their knees if she wished it."

Frost's face pinched.

He wouldn't look at me.

"I don't though," I said, butting in, feeling like I should just throw that out there. "I *don't* want them."

"But you want Azrael?" Frost barked, making me flush with embarrassment and rage at the same time.

I didn't reply, not trusting myself not to bark right back at him.

"Come on, man," Ethan said, ever the level-headed one. "You were just saying yesterday how he wasn't as bad as we thought."

Frost grumbled something unintelligible to himself.

"Besides," Blake added with a shrug. "If the most

powerful vampire blood mated to her, would that really be so bad? More protection for her not just until the end of this war, but if Az sticks around then maybe forever. Or at least, for the rest of her life."

He just *had* to add that bit to the end, didn't he?

I suppressed a groan, stifling the growing feeling of unease in my belly.

Frost relaxed, if only a little, and I got the distinct feeling it was the mood shift in the room at the mention of my impending demise due to old age than it was to do with anything else Blake had said.

I stood, unable to stand this conversation, or being in this room any longer. "Look," I snapped, letting the anger flow hot and ready through my veins. I would *not* be made to feel like a damned hoe because of how I felt. "If you don't like the idea then it won't happen. Period. Happy?"

Frost's eyes widened at that and he took a step back as though struck by the words.

He didn't reply.

"Good," I said, voice dripping sarcasm as I stepped into my leather boots and nearly ripped the laces to pieces trying to tie them. "Now that's over with. I'm going to go work out. After that, I'm probably going to check on Azrael. *Check on him* not *fuck him*, in case that wasn't clear."

I was being a bitch and I knew it, but I didn't care. I shouldered past Frost on my way out the door, body radiating heat.

It was true what I said, I wouldn't do anything they were uncomfortable with, even if it was only one of them that didn't want me to be with Az. I had my guys. I loved my guys. Wasn't that enough?

I resolved to not give in to my feelings for Az, lifting my chin as I strode toward the gym, ready to rip what was left of the training dummies apart. Hoping that my resolve alone would be strong enough to control myself because if I knew anything, it was that being around Azrael made me *want* to lose control.

And fuck if it wasn't easy to slip.

6

I destroyed what remained of the training dummies. And half of the gym equipment too. There was no telling how long I'd been in there, taking out my frustration, my fear, my *guilt* on everything in the room. But at some point, Ethan inched the door open and very slowly stepped inside to place a tray of still lightly steaming rice and curry on the half busted weight lifting bench. Setting a massive bottle of water next to it.

He didn't make eye contact with me as he cleared his throat and muttered to give Frost some time to come around before he left me alone again. My jaw had twitched in fury at first, but then my eyes betrayed me a long, stinging burn and the well of hot tears.

Didn't he get it?

It wasn't about that. It wasn't that Frost didn't want

to share me. I fucking *loved* him for not wanting to share me.

I hated myself for *wanting to be shared* by someone who wasn't my guys. I hated myself for allowing these emotions to take root in the first place.

Azrael was one of the two oldest vampires in the world. He'd admitted to torturing people. To killing thousands of innocents. To slaughtering and maiming and compelling whatever he wanted from whoever he wanted it from. I should hate him more than any of the other bloodsuckers I've killed.

But I don't.

I can't.

And it makes me want to rip him apart for making me feel this way. Almost as much as I want to rip off his clothes and fuck him stupid.

My muscles ached, twitching as I polished off the bottle of water.

My craving for curry had been ruined though. I barely finished half of it. Not even able to taste it.

The bastards *ruined* my curry.

Fucktards.

I bristled as a chill crept over my exertion warmed muscles as the heat began to leech out. But it was more than that. This *place* was really getting to me. The walls seemed to be creeping in by the inch every hour. Soon, they would crush me. I had no doubt.

I needed to get out. I needed air. *Real* air. Not this recycled bullshit.

The guys, all the vampires really, didn't *need* to breathe. I did.

My lungs felt tight. Constricted.

Maybe if I asked *really* nicely Azrael would let me go out. Just for an hour.

I almost laughed at myself just for having the doomed hope. As if.

Sighing, I rolled my shoulders back, sufficiently sated from beating everything in the room to a pulp and set off to find Azrael.

His door was shut, and no light shone out from the bottom. Inside there's no sound but I can sense him in there. A dark presence lurking in the shadows.

This time he didn't invite me in, and a jolt of worry ricocheted down my spine. I hated myself for it.

"Az?" I hedged, clearing my throat as I tentatively pushed the door open.

My eyes struggled to adjust to the change in light and I fumbled on the wall, searching for a light switch. "Azrael? Are you— "

"Don't," he warned just as my finger brushed the plastic switch. "The light—it burns."

Cursing, I shut the door behind me, sealing out the little bit of light creeping in from the hall.

"What is it?" He asked, and I stutter for words, feeling like a fucking idiot all of a sudden. Why did I even bother to check up on him? He's a big boy.

Mattress coils creaked and a muted groan betrayed his pain.

Steeling myself, I strode toward him, able to make out the outlines of objects in my path enough to avoid them and pick my way to Azrael's bed.

"You need some more," I told him more than asked, feeling the edge of the bed, and sitting down on it. So close to him I could feel the lightest touch of his body heat.

I found his arm and trailed my fingers up it, finding him laying back against a mound of pillows on the headboard. I could just make out the shape of him in the dark, but barely. My human eyes, though better than any other humans, were no match for vampire vision. He could probably see me perfectly.

When my fingers found his neck, and then his jaw, I leaned in, exposing my neck to him.

Azrael's hands found my body, reaching up to brush over my neck, leaving a trail of fire everywhere they touched. Until he eventually settled them on either side of my face, cupping my jaw. I got the distinct sense he was studying me in the dark and felt strangely vulnerable even though I couldn't see his eyes in the dim.

"No," he replied, his voice a deep rumble in his chest, though the way his fingers tightened infinitesi-mally as he said that one word gave away how badly he wanted to.

"Don't be stubborn."

His thumb brushed over my chin, and then a second later, my lower lip, making my womb clench. Warmth spread like poison down to my throbbing pussy. Scattered through my veins like shockwaves.

Oh god.

Fuck.

I dropped my hands to the silken sheets, fisting them in the soft, rumpled fabric.

"You need your strength," I argued, turning my head back to the side, twisting out of his grasp. His hands fell from my face. "If something were to happen— "

"Nothing will happen. This place is safe."

"Azrael," I all but shouted. "I *want you* to take it. Just enough to finish healing."

I could tell he was still in pain. Much more than Ethan was. I was no scientist, but I could speculate the reason why.

His age.

Time made vampires stronger, but it also made them more vulnerable to the sun. A baby vampire took minutes to fully go up in flame and be reduced to ash.

An ancient vampire…well, I didn't have a lot to go on, but I'd once seen one that was over a century year old go up in smoke within about a minute. Maybe forty seconds.

Azrael was more hurt than he was letting on. I'd bet money on it.

His hands reached out once more, tentatively this time, brushing my hair away from my neck with one while the other gripped a fistful of my hair and then I was on my back, pressed flat against his bare chest as he yanked my head to one side, and I felt the brush of his lips on my throat.

My pulse soared, and laid atop him, I could feel the press of his semi against my tailbone as he hardened in his pants.

Shit.

Control.

I am in control.

"And you call me stubborn," he murmured against my neck, tongue flicking out to taste me.

I was about to tell him to stop playing and just take it already when every sane and rational thought was expunged from my mind. His fangs slid into my neck slow and easy. This was no feral bite. It was something else.

As his fangs pushed into me, their venom flooding my veins like a drug, I squirmed in his lap, a gasping moan tripping from my lips.

Azrael's arm came around me like a bar, securing me against him as he drank from my carotid.

I ground my ass against his cock, trying to move my arms but it was no use, he was too strong, and I couldn't break free. Didn't really want to.

He growled against my throat as I continued the circular motions with my hips and his hand around my ribcage moved up, pawing my right tit instead. I moaned as he tweaked the nipple, almost lost to the venom now.

My pussy slick. Pulse racing. Body a conductor of desire.

This was exactly what I was supposed to *not* let happen.

The thought was enough to sober me for the instant I needed to get myself under control.

Az stiffened beneath me and I knew without needing to ask that he'd heard my thoughts. Had rooted out the reason why I was resisting the venom's call.

He released me at once and I slid from his lap, breathless and shaking all over from the rush. I put my head between my knees to stop the stars from exploding in my vision.

"I understand," he said in a whisper while I continued trying to catch my breath and regain composure. "If you were mine, I wouldn't want to share you, either."

I was grateful he didn't mention the other bit. The part about my having feelings for him. I'd never allowed myself to think it before, but there it was. Cards on the table.

At least...mine were.

He was still playing his close to the chest.

Didn't matter anyway.

It would be better if I were just a plaything to him, then it would be easier to keep apart.

"How do you feel?" I asked when I finally caught my breath, eager to change the subject and red-faced and trying to hide it by keeping my head tilted away from his watchful gaze.

He paused before answering. "Better. I can feel what remained of the injury healing."

Then this wasn't all a massive waste of energy. Good.

I realized that I should probably leave, but the truth was that I didn't want to. Here in the dark with Azrael distracting me I could pretend I wasn't in a bunker below ground. Once I left this room, I'd have to face the walls again.

His hand pressed against my back and I stiffened beneath his touch before realizing, confusedly, that it was a comforting gesture. When he finally spoke a moment later his voice was strained.

"You need to leave," he said. Not a question, but I knew he wanted me to confirm, nonetheless.

I nodded, knowing he would be able to see the small movement.

"If I could just go outside for an hour…"

His hand vanished from my back and a light flicked on, momentarily blinding me.

I blinked, cringing as my eyes adjusted and the walls pressed in again.

Azrael opened a drawer next to the bed, lifting up a false bottom and drawing out something small on a silver chain. I tried not to notice how fucking delicious he looked wearing nothing but a pair of boxers hanging low on his hips. Paying attention instead to what he was holding in his hands as he held it out to me.

I took the smooth pearlescent stone and the chain it hung on, my eyes going wide as I saw the unmistakable spark of something swirling within the stone. It was magic.

"What is it?"

"It's an ancient form of magic. It's purified bind-stone imbued with magic."

"It's…*what?*"

Azrael's lips pressed together.

"What does it do?"

"It's what I was looking for while you and the others travelled here. I knew I'd need a way to leave the bunker undetected to gather anything we might need and get intel from my watchdogs."

Was he saying this was what I thought it was?

"Wait a second, you can just put this on, and then Amala can't find you?"

Azrael nodded grimly, his eyes darkening. Meanwhile, my mind whirred with possibility.

"Well can we get more? If we had enough for all of— "

Azrael shook his head, silencing me. "No. The type of magic used to make this stone was lost a very long time ago. Only a few of these remain and the witches who carry them do not share their power with other immortals."

"Then how did you get this one?"

He waited for me to understand instead of replying, and I realized at once that I already did.

He *killed* a witch to get this stone.

From the sounds of it a very powerful witch.

Too bad it wasn't that bitch Amala, then we wouldn't need to hide at all. The two-timing cunt was the reason I'd been captured in the first place. Faking her loyalty to Azrael while going back to her true master, Raphael, the entire time.

Though something about the whole situation didn't sit right with me. She hadn't told Raphael about the house in Italy. She hadn't told him about the army we'd already begun amassing. It was possible she didn't know about it, even though it was happening right under her nose, but that wasn't all.

Unless I imagined it, Amala had also given me the chance to escape in New York. She *lied* to Rafe about Luz being pregnant to ensure he didn't kill me right there and then. Thus, giving me the opportunity I needed to escape.

Azrael cocked his head at me, and I knew he was also puzzling through my thoughts. "Interesting," he murmured, but said nothing else, a line forming between his brows.

"Do you think she could be playing him, too?" I asked, voicing what I'd been wondering since she helped me that day.

His lips tightened. "I'm not sure. As you likely already know, witches don't generally consort in vampire affairs. Or in affairs with any of the other immortal species."

I did know that. They thought themselves above all the others. They didn't share their magic and they were quick to snuff out any that would see them toppled from their thrones. Or that would see us outed to the mortal public.

"But Amala doesn't follow the laws of the witch's council, right? She's a rogue."

He nodded slowly.

"I'm not sure what her game is, but it's better to remain out of her sight."

Azrael inclined his head to the necklace. "You may use it to leave the bunker. I trust that you will be inconspicuous and cautious."

"I will."

"And that you will not go far from these walls and will only leave during daylight hours and return before the sun sets."

I couldn't help the raw emotion bursting up from within me at his demands. I didn't care what I had to do. *I could leave.* I'd wear a fucking bubble suit if I had to. I'd wear a tracking device and riot helmet and a body cam. Just let. Me. Out.

Az's face cracked into a half grin at my inner monologue. "Don't tempt me, kitten. I just might make you do all of that and more."

Unable to stop myself, I flung my arms around him, burrowing my face in his chest. Inhaling deep lungsful of his heady scent. "Thank you," I muttered, the words muffled against his flesh.

He stroked the back of my head in what could almost be called a return embrace before he pulled back.

The char on his face was almost entirely gone now and his eye, the one that had been more affected was nearly back to a clear white, most of the red tongue and angry veins gone.

"It's only fair," he said with a sigh, rising to dig through a mound of clothes on an armchair against the wall and drawing out a pair of rumpled jeans. "You helped me. Now it's my turn to do something for you."

Fair enough.

I jumped from the bed, practically bouncing on my heels in my haste to leave, even though there was one thing I wanted to take care of before I went outside.

"Rose," Azrael's suddenly hardened tone stopped me, and I whirled back around before I could reach the door.

He buttoned his jeans, body tense and jaw taut. Something like fire flashed in his eyes and I cringed inwardly at the sight, the warmth of excitement quickly turning to ice in my blood.

"Don't make me regret this."

It was as much a threat as it was a plea.

"I won't."

7

*A*s much I wanted to *run* straight outside without looking back, there was still a fair few hours before sunrise and I knew exactly how I wanted to spend that time. I may have promised the guys that I wouldn't act on my feelings for Azrael, and I hadn't.

But *someone* needed to take care of the fire he'd stirred within me. My panties were still wet with the arousal from his bite. And his touch. I mean, it was only fair that if I couldn't do anything about what I felt that they be the ones to quench the thirst.

To suffocate the flames.

Right?

Besides, I really doubted they would mind.

I swept into the room a moment later, finding Blake alone, looking bored as fuck at the desk. The office chair propped back so that he could rest his crossed ankles on the desktop as he twirled a short blade between his thumb and forefinger.

Distantly, I could hear the shower running in the bathroom, but I could only sense two of them in here. And I could guess who was missing.

"You look better," Blake offered, kicking his feet back down to the floor. "Frost said you did a number on the training room."

I gave a half shrug in reply. "Where is he?"

"Don't know. He left a few minutes after you did. Hasn't come back except to grab a change of clothes."

So, it was Ethan in the shower then.

There weren't many places in the bunker that Frost could be. Our wing of it consisted of the lab, our bedrooms, the training room, some storage, and a sad cafeteria. There wasn't much else. And he wasn't stupid enough to go hang out with the recruits in the other side of the bunker.

Was he?

I shook off the worry eating at me and got back down to business.

Frost could go be by himself and pissy all he wanted.

I mean, he did *get* what he wanted anyway; me all to himself and the guys, not to be shared with anyone else. If anyone should be pissy, really it shouldn't be him. He should be glad I have no interest in becoming a vampire queen and taking a hundred or more blood mates.

"I take it back," Blake said with a sly grin. "You look pissed off again."

I rolled my eyes, sighing. I didn't want to talk about it anymore right then. We could worry about this shit later. I could worry about Frost *later*.

"I need a shower," I said, dropping the necklace onto the bedside table and unzipping my pants. I could tell them all about the necklace *after*.

I got the distinct feeling it would only lead to another fight I didn't want to have yet, anyway. As if they would actually believe a necklace would be enough to safeguard me while I went outside without them for a few hours.

Yeah. I would totally deal with that once I'd solved this very prominent problem first.

The moment my pants dropped to the ground, Blake's eyes grew heavy, perhaps scenting my arousal now that the leathers weren't covering it.

"Ethan is in there," Blake replied in a husky whisper, biting hard on his lower lip as I shucked off what remained of my clothing and tossed my boots to the floor.

I gave him a sly look and popped my hip, giving him a full and unobstructed view of my wet pussy. "I know."

Blake's eyes darkened and he pawed at the growing bulge beneath his tight dark jeans.

"You coming?" I asked before striding past him

toward the door to the bathroom. "I could use some help washing my back."

Clothing rustled behind me, and just as I opened the door, he caught up to me. His hard length pressed into my lower back as he pulled me flush against him. My arms were pinned to my breasts and my feet left the ground, his deep growl reverberating through my chest. The sound ignited my nerve endings, and I bit my lip to keep from moaning.

"Blake?" Ethan called through the steam.

"I caught an intruder trying to sneak in." Blake's voice was low and gruff, and I shuddered with need.

Ethan's head popped out of the shower, his expression morphing from battle-ready to a heated gaze as he took in my naked body, his cheeks and ears already flushed from the hot water. His eyes hungrily followed Blake's hand as it trailed down my stomach. Heat pooled in my belly as he wordlessly opened the shower door wide enough for Blake to carry me through. The crisp nautical scent of his body wash surrounded us.

"What should we do with her?" Ethan asked once the door slid shut behind us.

The corner of his mouth tilted up at Blake's game and I wanted those lips on mine, but my captor held tight. Blake's nose brushed through my hair, then down across my shoulder. I prepared myself for his directions. Even though I hated following orders, his control during sex was a fucking huge turn-on.

"Hmm." He set me down on the slick floor carefully. "I think she should be on her knees."

Ethan's eyes flicked to mine briefly, long enough for me to make my own will known. I wanted my guys any way I could get them. They wouldn't let me down. I would get mine soon enough, after Blake had his fun.

I sank to the floor, mouthwatering at the sight of the fully erect cocks on either side of me. The hot water ricocheted from Ethan's shoulders, coating me in the soft mist. Taking them in each hand, I gave a tentative stroke. Blake watched with heavy eyes and Ethan hissed, grabbing the wall to steady himself. If they thought I was the helpless prey in this vulnerable position, I would prove them wrong. I would bring them to their knees with me.

My grip tightened on Blake as Ethan's massive length slid down my tongue, touching the back of my throat. He grunted, squeezing his eyes shut as I pulled my head back and did it again. I ran my tongue around the ridge of his head and across his slit, then turned to Blake.

It took more to get a reaction from him. He could tell by my mischievous grin that I was aiming for one and I saw the amusement around his eyes, but even he couldn't hold out long. I wrapped my tongue around his length, increasing the suction, and took him all the way in.

"Fuck, Rose," he growled, his fingers curling into

my slightly damp hair. His hips rocked into me and I moaned around him.

I moved back and forth between them, alternating between my mouth and my hands but keeping up a pace. Each time I took Ethan into my mouth, I grabbed his ass and pulled him closer until I had them both practically right on top of me. When I released him, his eyes half-lidded as he watched, I pulled my guys together.

Blake's jaw fell open, realizing what I meant to do just before I did it, but it was too late. I took them in one hand, pressing their dicks together, then took both of them into my mouth. Blake's hand smacked down on the shower wall beside Ethan's.

His reaction gave me a primal satisfaction and, with one hand freed up, I sought my own release. The taste, the *feel* of them together in my mouth was almost as addictive as their venom. Blake and Ethan groaned, the pressure intensifying for both of them. They were almost there, I could feel it, could see it in their strained expressions.

My fingers circled my aching wet sex.

Fuck, I wanted to feel them both cum at the same time.

Wanted to bring them down.

But then Blake grabbed my head and pulled away, Ethan following his lead. Disappointment must've shown in my face because Ethan pulled me to my feet and locked his lips to mine. I went to grab his cock again, but my arms were pulled behind my back.

"Taking some pretty creative liberties now, are we?" Blake purred into my ear.

I leaned back into him as much as I could. "Don't pretend you didn't like it."

Blake nodded his head over my shoulder, pulling me back further and trapping my arms against his hard stomach. "Ethan."

The breath left my lungs when Ethan's strong fingers slid between my legs. I tried to move, to grind against him, but Blake clamped down around my belly.

"Hold very still," he said, his heavy breaths hot on my skin, on my ear. "Ethan is going to make you cum, then, and only then, we might give you what you came in here for."

Shit. I wasn't sure how still I could be with Ethan's fingers swirling expertly. He stepped close, nearly pressed flush against me, and took my lips again. Blake kept one arm across my stomach, the other gliding up to caress my breast and pinch my nipple.

I fought the urge to squirm as sparks of desire crackled across my skin. Water dripped from Ethan's hair and his lips moved against mine, his unique taste flooding my system. The orgasm I'd been wanting since Azrael fed from me built up rapidly.

Dammit. The thought of the ancient vampire was exactly what I didn't need right then. I didn't need to remember how hard he was beneath me, how much I'd wanted him despite what I'd just told Frost. How fucking hot he was in nothing but boxers.

How he'd tried to comfort me, even if it was in such a tiny gesture.

I was suddenly glad my guys couldn't read minds the way Azrael could, and I felt a bit guilty for thinking of him while I was with them. Ethan's tongue disappeared from my mouth and he pulled away enough to meet my gaze. My breaths were coming more rapidly as I approached the edge, his and Blake's loving attention undoing me.

"Bite me," I whimpered, trying my damnedest to keep still. "Please."

His eyes met Blake's and some kind of silent message must have passed between them because he disappeared, dropping to his knees. Blake nudged my head to the side with his and I exposed my throat to him eagerly. Ethan spread my legs, taking me into his mouth.

"Fuck!"

I gasped, the difference in sensation between his fingers and tongue incredible. My toes curled and my core trembled beneath my restraint, my breath becoming harder to catch. Ethan blinked water from his eyelashes as he watched my reactions, his steeped-tea eyes dark with arousal.

"Fucking do it!"

Blake grabbed my throat as his fangs sunk into my neck the same time Ethan's entered my inner thigh.

The world shattered around me as their venom took hold, mixing with the remnants of Azrael's and throwing me into a free fall over the edge. My moans bounced off the shower walls, but it wasn't enough.

It wasn't enough until they were inside me. I wanted to feel them, wanted them to follow me over that blissful horizon.

As if they knew the direction of my thoughts, Ethan drew back and stood, positioning himself at my entrance. Blake's fangs retracted as well and he adjusted his grip on me, angling my body for Ethan to enter me.

"Both," I said through the haze of pleasure. I couldn't have it any other way now. As long as my guys were with me, I would have them all in me. Filling me to the brim.

"You'll get both, love," Blake murmured in my ear.

Ethan wrapped my legs around his waist and eased in slowly, letting me adjust to him. I didn't want slow, though. I just fucking *wanted*.

Once he was seated, he got a good grip on my hips and thrust a few times. The delicious friction threatened to throw me over again, but he stopped. Before I could ask what they were doing, Blake's grip changed. They leaned me back carefully, Blake keeping hold of my shoulders.

Holy fuck.

His proud cock stood before me and I reached back, glancing up at him for permission. He nodded and, without an ounce of hesitation, I grabbed his tight ass and took him into my mouth. My legs tightened around Ethan as he and Blake both started thrusting, each from different ends. I knew they wouldn't drop me, despite the warm water pouring over us.

The angle they held me at was perfect for the three of us. Blake's cock slid right down my throat without issue, and Ethan was slamming into the most exquisite spot that had another orgasm working its way to the forefront. I only wished Frost was there with us to complete it.

Ethan's grip shook, his breaths coming in short pants as he stiffened further inside me. I moaned around Blake's cock, urging them on, begging them to come with me as my muscles contracted and I tumbled once more into a dizzying euphoria. Blake's hips jerked unevenly, and he made a half-whispered noise as he came, heat splashing against the back of my throat. Ethan was only a couple strokes behind him, his grip nearly bruising as he drove deep and hard, filling me with all of him.

Warmth flooded through me, and not just the physical kind.

There was so much love between us. Between all three of us. We knew it, were aware on another level how much we loved each other. But I'd only managed to say the words to one of them.

Now wasn't the time, though. The words seemed somehow less genuine in the heat of sex. I would tell them, though. They deserved that much from me before this was all over.

THE HOT WATER ran out not long after we'd finished, prompting me to wash up the fastest I think I ever had before. Somehow it managed to be hellishly uncomfortable, but also wildly reinvigorating at the same time.

I couldn't remember the last time I forced myself into an ice bath, but I certainly only did it when it was absolutely necessary. When the bruises and fractures were too many to count and all I could hope for was some numbness and to reduce the swelling while my body healed.

Cold showers weren't even half as bad as that. Ethan and Blake had laughed at me the whole time, the bastards immune to the cold just as they were to most everything else.

I had to begrudgingly admit it. There were *some* perks to being a vampire.

"So, explain to me again how that necklace is supposed to protect you?" Ethan asked, his face a mask of discomfort even though he was clearly trying to remain calm.

"Not protect me, exactly. More like *shield* me. As long as I'm wearing it Amala won't be able to track me."

"I don't like it," Blake added, scrubbing a palm over his jaw. "I think it's a bad idea."

"I'm sorry Rose, but I think I'm with Blake on this."

"Can't you just go and poke your head out for a bit? Why do you actually need to *leave*?"

I groaned, frustrated with having to explain myself. They couldn't understand because they didn't suffer the same way I did down here. "I could," I replied. And it would help a little bit. Hell, just going and sitting cross legged outside for an hour would help a massive amount, but not as much as it would help to actually *move*.

To run in wide open space beneath the sky. To drive with the windows down. To feel the rush of wind over my skin. Be around real living, breathing human beings. I wasn't meant to be caged. My body ached for freedom.

Going halfway might help, but the claustrophobic feelings would only return the moment I stepped back down those steps into the bunker.

"But it wouldn't help enough?" Ethan asked, trying to understand.

I shook my head.

"And it doesn't matter. Whether I just sit up there under the sun for an hour or go for a ride into town, the necklace will shield me from Amala, and the sun will protect me from the reach of other vampires. So, what's the difference."

Blake pursed his lips.

"Frost will be pissed if we let you go."

"Frost can suck a goat."

Ethan tilted his head, brows crinkling at my weak attempt at insult.

"Look, I'm going to go. If Azrael says it should be safe, then I believe him. And do you really think he would let me go if he didn't believe that himself?"

They had no argument for that.

"I'll be careful. I'll go straight into town. Grab some food. Maybe a nice big bottle of Stolichnaya to bring back with me, and I'll come straight back. I'll be here long before sundown. I promise."

The truth was that I was kind of hoping I could catch wind of some naughty vampires in the area while I was out. My fingers itched to stake and slice. I doubted I'd be able to catch any on the hunt, it being daylight and all, but I could still get lucky. I could stumble across a den. Take them out before they could even fully wipe the sleep from their eyes.

"Why do I feel like you're lying," Blake asked, his shoulders squaring. "You *want* a fight. I can see it in your eyes."

"I—" I tripped over a response. "Fuck. *Fine.* I'll just go and get some motherfucking air and not have any fun at all and then I'll come back. Happy?"

"Satisfied."

"She shouldn't do this. It isn't safe."

"I'm right here," I hissed, turning to find Ethan looking at me funny.

"I didn't say anything?"

103

A hand grabbed my upper arm, and my gaze was dragged back to Blake. "Did you just…?"

I jerked my arm away. "I can't control it yet, but… yeah. I can hear some thoughts now. Don't freak out or anything. It's not like I'm going to barge into your every thought like someone else we know."

I couldn't promise anything though. The few times it'd happened so far, it'd been wholly outside of my control and I didn't even know what caused it.

"Do you think breaking Rafe's compulsion…" Ethan trailed off and I could see that he was thinking a million miles a minute in that big head of his even though as much as I tried, I couldn't hear anything he was thinking now that I was actually *trying* to.

"What? Like it unlocked something in my head?"

Ethan's faraway gaze fell back to me. "Something like that."

"It felt a lot more like putting my brain—and the rest of my insides—in a blender for hours at a time, but maybe. I can't think of any other reason why I'd be able to now when I couldn't before."

I caught a glimpse of the time on Ethan's watch and almost squealed when I realized the sun should already be up and perky in the sky.

"Have you tested this with Az yet? Maybe you can stop his compulsion now."

I dropped my head and sighed, pinching the bridge of my nose. "Can we talk about this when I come back?"

My blood was buzzing with the need to leave now.

"Maybe we could use some of the elixir and come with you?" Ethan asked, but by the way he asked it, lower lip between his teeth and hands stuffed deep into his pockets, even he knew that wasn't an option. Not unless he wanted to take even more of my blood to replace whatever they used.

We were already barely going to have enough to ink into the vampires' skin for them to withstand the sun as long as we needed them to.

"I won't go far," I promised, shoving down the urge to draw my claws and tell them to quick fucking babying me. I knew they were only saying everything they were because of how deeply they cared for me.

I stood on tip toe to press a soft kiss to Ethan's lips and did the same for Blake, who snagged me around the waist and forced my lips open with his tongue, stealing the breath from my lungs and making me dizzy before he set me back down.

"If you aren't back in three hours, I'm going to force Ethan to ink me and I'm coming to drag your ass back. Got it?"

"He won't have to force me," Ethan interjected.

"Okay," I replied, breathless as he fully released me. "I got it."

GODDAMN ALPHA MALES. Why wasn't I attracted to the sweet, innocent ones? Why was it always the

ELENA LAWSON

psychopaths? I giggled to myself, resolving that Ethan was close enough to being one of those 'sweet guys' provided you didn't piss him off or threaten anyone he cared about. Then he was absolutely lethal. Feral.

There was a reason he took the longest to learn how to control his thirst for blood.

When I didn't run into Frost at all on my way out of the bunker, I had to grapple with warring emotions of disappointment and relief. I wasn't ready to talk to him yet, but I also didn't like the distance he was putting between us. It hurt.

Just another thing to add to the ever-growing list of things to fix *later*. After this war. After we had our vengeance, and the world was purged of Raphael's particular brand of evil.

A jingle behind me as I reached the final door put me on high alert and I had both stakes drawn from the concealed holsters on the outside of my boots before I even turned around.

Azrael tossed the keys to me and I caught them on my pinkie finger, giving him a questioning look. A little unsettled that I didn't feel his presence there behind me until I heard him.

"There's a small shed outside. The small key will open the lock. The other is for the motorcycle inside."

I arched a brow.

"I made some calls last night. Had it delivered. The nearest town is twenty-five miles away and I want you back here as fast as possible."

"The guys already gave me a time limit."

"Oh?"

"Three hours or they'll come after me."

His eyes narrowed.

"I'll give you two."

I rolled my eyes.

"Okay *dad*."

I opened my mouth to say something else, but he was already gone. Vanished the way he'd come, leaving only a soft breeze and his scent behind.

"Great," I muttered to myself. Now I only had *two* hours of freedom.

But fuck if I wasn't damn near about to break out into song at the idea of climbing on the back of a bike and *flying* the hell out of here.

I twirled the keys on my finger after re-sheathing my stakes and practically skipped out into the cold light of a late Canadian morning. I shut the garage-style door behind me, skin bristling at the chill in the air and lungs practically fucking orgasming at the beauty of so much *air*.

Clean air.

Air that smelled of cool pine and the threat of snow on the horizon.

Immediately my hyper tensed shoulders relaxed, and I took my time wandering to the small shed Az indicated, taking in the distance of the sky. The expanse of wooded land on all sides of me, and the long gravel drive leading out the compound gates and away to freedom.

I'd been so distracted the other day when the vampires met the sun, I'd hardly been able to enjoy it myself for more than a second. I'd be damned if I wasn't going to enjoy it this time.

"Oh, fuck yes," I said excitedly as the door to the shed fell away to reveal the monster of a bike crouched within, begging to be ridden.

I was going to enjoy the absolute hell out of it this time.

Twenty-five miles Az had said?

I was willing to bet I could clear that in twenty minutes flat on the navy-blue Ducati.

"I shall call you Hellhound."

8

---

*S*o, it took more like twenty-three minutes, but all in all, I was pretty damn impressed, both with the bike and myself. I parked him near a quiet downtown strip, removing my helmet and latching it to the back. I pressed two fingers to my lips and then to the bike. "I'll be back for you."

"What is she wearing?"

I heard the whisper from half a block down the street as a young girl unlocked the front door of a coffee shop, letting herself and another girl inside.

"Is there a Comic-Con in town that we don't know about?" The other replied, laughter ringing in her sarcastic tone.

And fuck if it didn't set my skin crawling.

I hadn't exactly been leading my regular life these past few months. I hadn't even thought about my clothes. In my fighting leathers and tall black boots, I probably did look like a fucking superhero wannabe.

Not exactly *inconspicuous*.

Steeling myself, I rushed down the street, calling to the two girls in their late teens or maybe early twenties. They were just the right size for my tiny frame though.

"Excuse me," I said, halting them before they could lock the door behind themselves to get started for the day.

"The convention center is *that* way," the one with the bleach blonde hair told me, pointing a polished finger in the direction I'd just come.

...and I thought Canadians were supposed to be nice?

"Sasha don't be rude," the other girl chastised her friend and then turned to me. "Do you need help finding something?"

"Is it that obvious I'm not from here?"

She shrugged with a hesitant smile, her eyes alighting on the handle of the blade at my hip. Hopefully, she thought it was just a part of my 'costume', but I didn't much care either way. They weren't going to remember this.

"Can I come inside?"

The blonde's eyebrows wrinkled. "No, we aren't even open— "

"Let me inside," I deadpanned, letting my compulsion flood the words. "I need to borrow some clothes."

Even though I'd have much preferred the jeans, fitted black tee, and long trench-like jacket of the brunette, I gestured for the blonde to take off her ugly ass purple sweatshirt and plaid black and white skirt. She was the ruder of the two and deserved it more.

"Now, it seems you've forgotten your clothes at home. Maybe your friend can lend you her jacket while you go home and get dressed."

The blonde nodded, her face turning crimson as she pulled on her friend's fitted trench coat and belted it at the waist before rushing out the door.

I went behind the counter and grabbed a plastic bag, stuffing my leathers inside it and feeling ridiculous as the fuzzy material of the sweater itched my skin. "Whoever said kindness doesn't pay was dead wrong," I muttered, walking past the dazed brunette and back out the fresh air. "Have a nice day!"

"You too," she called after me, blinking out of the haze of my compulsion as the door shut, leaving her to ready the tiny shop by herself. I was sure she'd manage.

I huffed, tipping my head to one side to crack my neck, rubbing out a kink there while I took another glorious lungful of fresh air. Twirling the gemstone between my fingers for a moment, I silently thanked whatever magic made this outing possible and then dropped it back down the front of my sweater, letting it rest against my warm breasts.

A creeping sensation rushed up my spine not a full block of walking later and I carefully checked the reflections in the glass windows of the shops to either side of me. Using only my peripherals and the reflections. Not daring to turn.

It wasn't the feel of a vampire, which was really too bad—it was something else. A simpler feeling.

The sensation of being watched.

It's daylight, I reminded myself.

It's probably just some douche canoe checking you out.

Regardless, I continued to check the reflections as I wandered through the little town in search of a liquor store and something half decent to eat. The strange creeping feeling didn't ease. Not after I ate a footlong sub on the park bench near the edge of the town. Not after I compelled myself a 60 of Stolichnaya from the local pub because I couldn't find a liquor store. And not when I finally made my way back to Hellhound with hardly thirty minutes to spare to get myself back to the bunker.

"Fucking hell," I cursed beneath my breath as I dipped into one last shop and fingered a little hello-kitty backpack off a hook by the door to stuff my vodka and leathers into. I wasn't going to have time to change back into them if I expected to make it back in time.

I pulled on the bag and got on Hellhound, pausing to take a good look around as I started his engine.

No one in the alleyways. No one in the windows of the second story apartments above the shops. Just *no one* watching me.

Was I being paranoid?

"Get your shit together, Rose," I growled, pissed off that my own paranoia was *ruining* this whole outing for me. I was on edge. Tense. And it was completely destroying my ability to enjoy even a second of it.

"There's no one there," I whispered, kicking up the stand with my heel to roll out of the parking space.

"Are you certain?"

The cool lilting tone sent shivers of recognition through me and I swiveled my head, stepping down to stop the forward trajectory of the bike. Past the early-bird shoppers, standing on the street corner like a sentinel was Amala.

I might not have even recognized her at first if I'd seen her earlier. In street clothes instead of her regular long dress and robe. Her hair twisted into a tight bun on the top of her head. Sporting...ripped jeans and some combat boots I'd have purchased myself.

She blended into the scenery around her like she was made from it, but we both knew she was cut from a different sort of cloth. And older than the onlookers passing her by could even imagine.

My hands tightened on the handlebars, my thoughts a twisted mess in my skull.

Impossible.

The necklace...

She shouldn't have been able to find me.

Immediately, I scanned the streets around her. The rooftops. The windows. Searching for any sign of lurking threats.

"I'm alone," she confirmed a second later, tentatively side-stepping a couple and their young daughter to make her way closer to me.

"Stay back," I warned, hand resting on the hidden stake tucked into the holster on my boot.

She halted, lifting a thin brow. "I've not come to hurt you, Rose. I'd like to talk."

"How did you find me?"

A man paused as he exited his car, glancing between Amala and I.

Amala flicked her fingers at her side and a little swirl of light expanded and dissipated in the blink of an eye.

The man blinked, and then walked away as though he'd never seen us.

"Neat trick," I commented, my teeth grinding so hard I thought they might crack. "Now how the hell did you find me?"

Amala cocked her head. "You do realize there are non-magical ways to track someone down if you know the right people, don't you?"

She must have seen the confusion play out in my features because she snorted, lacing her fingers together at her front before she explained.

"Azrael is good at tying up loose ends," she said. "But two planes leaving New York City in the middle of the night raises a few red flags. After that, it was simple to look up properties owned by Azrael's alias' in this area."

I gasped.

"I've known about the bunker since before you even arrived there."

No.

The guys.

Azrael.

I was up and off the bike, stake exchanged for the hooked blade at my hip, and in her face in half a second.

"What did you do? If you hurt them— "

"If I wanted them dead, they would be."

"Then what the fuck do you want? Why are you here."

A look of clear annoyance crossed her severe features, and she jutted her chin in the direction of the cafe I'd been inside earlier, just a little way down the block. "Five minutes. I want five minutes. And a latte."

"How do I know this isn't some sort of trap?"

My heart hammered behind my breastbone as I struggled to remember the interior of the cafe. The entrances and exits. Window locations. Good thing it was something I always checked whenever I entered a new place.

I knew there was an exit door at the back of the building and one large window next to the front entrance. I also knew that it was dark inside. Other than the front area where indirect sunlight illuminated the table closest to the door, it was dark enough for vampires to be without being burned up.

The guys would *kill* me if they knew I went in there with her.

I shouldn't go in there.

But a burning need to know what she wanted, and why she was out here alone ate at me from within. I had no doubt she was a formidable foe. One of the oldest witches in existence no doubt. Which would also make her extremely powerful.

But not even a witch could survive impalement by a metal stake.

Amala was the edge Rafe had over us. She was the reason we needed to hide out in that bunker in the first place. So that her magic couldn't track us.

An idea was forming in my mind and I wasn't sure if it was the most foolish thing I'd ever thought up, but it was pretty darn close.

"I could do an Americano," I shrugged, twirling my blade, and shoving it back into its holster. "Shall we?"

Amala warily eyed me, her bleached caramel gaze roving over my outfit with clear judgement.

"Nice sweater," she told me as she shouldered past and crossed the street, a smirk pulling at the corner of her mouth.

"Want to trade?" I joked, hoping my light tone concealed the murderous intent brewing in my core. I licked my lips, following her, searching for weak points.

My blood hummed with a singular focus I only got

during a hunt. This would be my most impressive conquest yet. If I succeeded.

"START TALKING," I demanded, on high alert but trying to hide it with slightly slouched shoulders and ankles crossed beneath the table as I took a sip of my Americano. I'd give her one minute.

I wanted to at least enjoy my coffee that long before her blood spilled over the table and ruined the moment. I heard no sounds of advance from any nook or cranny of the building. And I'd taken a table just behind the occupied one at the front of the store, where a large, framed landscape of a fantasy forest on the wall to our left had a good reflective view of the tables behind us.

"Raphael is getting close to figuring out that Luz isn't pregnant and won't ever be."

My stomach dropped and I almost spit out the small amount of coffee still in my mouth, but I forced myself to swallow it down, clattering the mug back down onto the table with my upper lip curling back. I'd been terrified she was already dead. Now, somehow knowing she's alive both relieves and enrages me because there isn't a damn thing I can do to save her right now. We aren't ready.

"Why are you telling me this?"

"I thought you'd want to know. Time is wearing thin for her life and the lives of the others."

She was trying to bait me, I could see it now. But why? To what end?

"Amala," I all but growled. "What do you want?"

She leaned back in her chair, looking for all the world like a boho-chic librarian and not a hundreds-of-years-old witch. "I want what you want. A world *without* the stain of Raphael's influence."

My eyes narrowed.

"And helping him attempt to make tiny demon children is just part of that plan? Standing by while he rapes and uses innocent women is just what? A fucking— "

"Rose," Amala interrupted. "If you would do me the favor of shutting your mouth, I'll explain."

I want to carve her face into a fucking jack-o-lantern.

"What I'm about to tell you cannot leave this cafe."

I gritted my teeth but shut up, waiting for her to spill.

"Raphael has begun adding to his forces. He knows a battle is imminent and I fear even the advantage of the sun will not be enough to defeat him."

My brows wrinkled and my throat went dry. So, she did know what Ethan was doing in the lab back in Italy. *She knows everything.*

"How did you know— "

"We know more than you think," she interrupted, settling a hard stare on me. "You need to strike now, before Raphael can get any stronger. He's compelling vampires in droves to join him. He'll be unstoppable if he keeps this pace."

I wrinkled my nose, stomach roiling with hot, wretched bile. "Why are you telling me this?"

"I am part of a group of alchemists who...*oversee* the affairs of other immortals. We are watchers of sorts. Only intervening to tip the scales in our favor, which is why I've come to warn you."

My head was starting to hurt. What the fuck was this bitch saying?

"*We?*" I demanded. "How many are you?"

Another idea sparked and my eyes widened as I shot a hand across the table, gripping her wrist. "You could help us," I said, unable to conceal the hope from the words.

Witches were strong. Powerful. With a group of them on our side *and* the sun, we could put Rafe and his minions down for good. We could *destroy them.*

Amala jerked her hand from my grasp, upper lip curling as though the feel of my skin against hers was offensive.

"We do not involve ourselves."

"But you just said yourself that you don't want Rafe to win this fight. If you helped us— "

"We do not involve ourselves," she repeated.

"Why not just assassinate him yourself?" I argued, the pitch of my voice rising as wrath filled me. "He trusts you. You could end this whole thing with one little flick of your witchy fingers."

Amala frowned. "Then there would be an even greater battle. A war between immortal species that would no doubt spill onto mortal streets. That would no doubt claim countless mortal lives."

I sat back hard in the uncomfortable wooden chair, my mind still reeling. But at least in this regard her and I could agree.

The battle to be fought vampire against vampire would be bad enough. Mortals would no doubt be caught in the crossfire, but a bigger war. A war that could last years fought between species wasn't an option.

And if a witch killed a high-powered vampire in cold blood, it was a possibility. From what little I knew; the three species were already on shaky ground.

"How do I know you aren't lying to me?" I asked after a minute, remembering to check my blind spots again just in case this whole thing was in fact a trap. But still, no one came from behind to attack. No other witches. And I felt no vampires in any proximity.

"Read me," she offered, lowering her shoulders. "I won't fight you."

I quirked a brow, realizing she was giving me permission to read her mind.

"I can't control it yet," I admitted.

She pursed her lips, seeming to be mulling over something before she set her jaw and slid her open palm across the table. "Give me your hand."

"Um. No."

She fixed me with a withering stare. "Stubborn child," she hissed between gritted teeth, snatching my hand from my mug before I could register the movement. Bitch was *fast*.

Her grip around my wrist tightened and fuck me if I wasn't curious as a thread of pure magical light bloomed on her palm as she held it over mine. A symbol, pulsing with reddish light, made up of a hundred tiny lines and slashes almost like runes. She pushed it into my skin, and I gasped, feeling a tickle of electricity course through me. A burning sensation attacking the calloused flesh of my palm.

I retracted my hand, rubbing the still prickling flesh. "What did you do?"

"Helped," she said.

Only, she didn't say it.

Amala inclined her head and her voice was clear as day even though her lips did not move.

A spell to strengthen power of mind, she explained, and my lips fell open at the ease of reading her thoughts. *It will not last forever, but if you attack swiftly, it may aid you in the battle to come. For now, you may use it to find the truth in my mind.*

"Thought you *didn't interfere?*"

She smirked. *I won't tell if you don't.*

Focusing my energy, I attempted to dig into Amala's mind, but it was like slogging through mud. There were barriers everywhere. She was allowing me access to her mind, but only parts of it. Only what she wanted me to see.

Tentatively, I nudged at one of the walls and it began to buckle under my pressure. A smile lifted the corners of my mouth and I just knew that if I pushed harder—fuck, if I visualized a swinging bat—I could knock them all to the ground.

"*Rose*," Amala warned, and all at once I was forcibly ejected from her mind and I groaned as a lancing pain shot from my forehead over my skull and down the back of my neck.

"What the fuck," I hissed, catching a troubled look from the barista as she passed us to clear the front table. "How did you— "

"How do you think I am able to keep watch on Raphael? On Azrael?"

Duh. Of course, she would need to be strong enough to block them from her mind given that she was a duplicitous bitch with an agenda.

"You got what you needed."

She was right. I had gleaned the information I needed from rooting around in her mind, even if it was only the information she wanted me to see. But I'd seen a few other things, too. Perhaps things I shouldn't have.

What mattered though was that she was telling the truth. She was playing Rafe just as she'd been playing Az. But her endgame goal was clear. Tip the scales in Azrael's favor. Stop Raphael from succeeding at all costs.

It was why she had to switch sides. She needed to keep a closer watch on Rafe. And when he asked her to *acquire* me, she couldn't very well refuse. She'd been given the green light to facilitate the transfer. The group she was with—they wanted to see how far Rafe was willing to go.

They also didn't seem to give two shits whether I lived or died. In fact, they had been banking on Rafe killing me. They wanted me eliminated from the equation. But not before I served my purpose—starting this war.

A war that would mean the decimation of hundreds of vampires. A war that might see the filth of Raphael, and perhaps Azrael too, purged from the mortal lands.

I blinked at Amala, incredulous.

"What is Manifesto?" I asked, a coy smile curving my mouth.

Her carefully crafted mask crumbled for a fraction of a second before she had it back in place. I wasn't supposed to know that name.

"You'd do well to forget that, Rose," she said and something in her tone as she stood, draining her latte, made me shudder. "I'd hate to see anything happen to you."

"Nice talking to you too," I called after her as she left, only relaxing once the door swung shut behind her.

Well, shit. Things just got really fucking interesting.

—————

hey were so busy arguing when I got back to the bunker that they somehow didn't hear me lock up Hellhound and walk over the crunching gravel to the entrance.

It wasn't until I called through the metal door, "Incoming!" That they shut up.

I eased the door open about two feet, crouching to roll beneath it so I wouldn't flood the room with the sunlight.

The instant the rolling door clattered to the ground, they were on top of me.

"What the fuck, Rose?" Blake all but growled while Ethan circled me, searching for injury and Frost brooded with his arms crossed hard over his chest.

Azrael, strangely, was the only one who looked calm, and I realized he'd already gleaned everything he needed from my thoughts and was already working through it all. His expression perplexed as his mismatched eyes swept back and forth over the concrete floor at his feet.

Welp, guess the cats out of the bag.

I mean, it wasn't like I was actually going to keep anything Amala told me from them anyway. She could suck it. I wasn't about to keep a secret that big from my guys or Azrael and if she thought I was she was fucking mental.

On a whim, I threw up a wall, blocking my thoughts from Az before he could delve further. He snapped his head up to meet my gaze with a haughty stare as the others muttered threats about tying me to the bed for the rest of my life and never letting me out of their sight again.

"How?"

I could feel Azrael press against the wall I'd erected in my thoughts like he taught me. But this time, he didn't break it down. I held no illusions that if he gave it his all that he couldn't. I was sure he could, but it was damn gratifying to see him struggle, even a little bit.

I kept the wall in place, reinforcing it with more bricks and mortar.

This secret I'd keep to myself for no other reason than that I *could.*

"I learned some new tricks," I replied with a wink. "Aren't you proud of me?"

"What the hell are you talking about?" Ethan

demanded, uncharacteristically tense. His frustration clear.

"Rose had a little visit," Azrael explained, eyeing me warily as he spoke. "From Amala."

"What?" Frost roared. "Where is the bitch? Does she know where we are?"

"Were you followed?" Blake added, his eyes darkening and body going rigid as he turned with a glare for Azrael. "I thought you said that necklace would work?"

"It did."

"Clearly, it didn't," Ethan retorted, bending to retrieve the spilled contents of his tattoo bag from the floor. Another few minutes and I was sure they all would have been after me.

Looked like I got back just in time.

"We need to talk," I told them. "And you aren't going to like it."

"How soon can we have the amount of elixir we need?" Azrael asked Ethan an hour later in the lab as he got out the tools needed to take more of my blood.

"A few days?"

"You don't sound so sure," I interjected as he wrapped a rubber tie around my bicep and pulled it tight.

"I don't know. Less than a week though for sure."

"Will that be fast enough, do you think?" I asked

Azrael, who'd begun to pace the small section of free tile floor.

He lifted his eyes to mine and something in the way he looked at me made me uneasy.

"We know he's still in New York," I began, going over the facts. "And that he's banking on us *not* attacking him there because of the humans that would be caught in the crossfire."

"Right," Azrael agreed as Ethan slid the needle into my vein and blood filled the tube, spiraling into a blood bag. "He wants to have this war on his terms. He'll move to a playing field of his choosing when he's ready."

"So, then we have to attack him in the city, while he isn't expecting it."

Ethan's fingers faltered at my words and he nearly dropped the blood bag in his hands but caught it just in time before it took the needle out of my skin with it to the floor. "We can't attack there. There will be too many people."

"It's our only choice," I argued, trying to think of some way to make it work.

"That's not a bad idea," Azrael mused as the thought was still forming in my mind. I threw the wall back up, shooting him a glare.

Fuck, it was exhausting keeping that thing up all the time. I was going to have a migraine soon if I tried too much longer.

"What?" Frost asked, looked between Azrael

and me.

Frost's thoughts flowed from him like water and I couldn't help but pick them up.

Don't know what she sees in him.

It's just fucking, though. Maybe Eth is right, and she just needs to get it out of her system.

It's not like she was a damn virgin when I found her.

Jesus. Didn't we have bigger problems right now? *That* was what he was thinking about. Guys were just as bad as girls. Fucking worse.

I did my best to ignore Frost's inner chatter, clearing my throat. "A bomb."

"You want to blow up the building?" Ethan asked, brows lowering. "But those girls—Rafe's wives— "

"Don't call them that," I snapped, unable to help the words from falling out. I calmed myself with a breath and then continued. "No, I don't want to blow up the building. I can't with them inside it. Besides, too many would survive the blast and we'd risk killing too many bystanders on the streets."

Blake threw a hand through his tousled black hair, grimacing. "What do you mean then?"

"A bomb *threat*," I explained and watched the dawning crawl over their expressions.

"A bomb threat would have the streets in the area evacuated," Ethan said, filling in the blanks.

I nodded. "And then all we'd have to deal with is a potential swat team."

"That's easy enough to fix," Frost grudgingly joined

the conversation. "Just compel the swat team leader not to enter until we say so. They'll keep the rest of them away."

I grinned. "Perfect."

I caught Azrael sharing a look with Blake as Ethan swapped out the blood bag for another, silently apologizing to me with his eyes as he drained me. My body began to slump, and my head was getting fuzzy, but I wasn't about to complain. If I did, he would stop. And if he stopped, we wouldn't have the amount of blood we needed to take Raphael down.

Frost's icy eyes met Azrael's too and his jaw twitched. Ethan furtively glanced at the ancient vampire between tasks too.

What was going on?

"Um," I said, drawing out the sound. "Want to fill me in?"

Clearly there was something I was missing.

Ethan sighed and I followed his gaze back to Azrael.

He was watching me with an unreadable expression that made my belly flip.

"What?" I demanded. "Spit it the fuck out."

"You must stay here."

I'm sorry, *what*?

"I must have heard you wrong. Did you actually just tell me that you want me to *stay behind*?"

I glared at the other three with equal rage, pain twisting in my gut as I realized they were all in on this. That they all *agreed*.

"Think about it for a second, Rose," Ethan implored, but couldn't look me in the eye as he spoke. "If you fall into Rafe's hands again— "

"If you *die*—" Blake interrupted, his voice a dead monotone even though his thoughts were screaming inside of him.

I won't let that happen. She will live. Even if all of us fall, at least she'll survive this bullshit.

"*No*," I bellowed, rising from my seat on the metal table and yanking the IV needle from the crook of my elbow, sending an arcing spray of crimson over the floor. "Fuck you," I hissed.

"*Fuck all of you*. Trying to make this kind of decision for me? How fucking dare you."

I hated this. Something ate at me from the inside and it tasted suspiciously like acid. My head throbbed and my pulse was pounding in my temples.

Fucking traitors.

Fucking alpha assholes thinking they can control what I do, and I don't.

I swayed a little on my feet but shook my head to steady myself.

"Rose, you should sit." Ethan hedged and I felt the brush of his fingers on my elbow. Whirled out of his grasp.

"Don't touch me."

Pain was etched in his soft brown eyes, but he lowered his hand.

"We're only trying to keep you safe."

131

"It's not just about you," Azrael added from behind me and it took every ounce of my self-control not to go postal on his ass as I turned around. He was lucky my body was still recovering from the blood Ethan had just taken.

"Your blood is a weapon in the wrong hands. If Rafe figured out how to create the same elixir as Ethan just think of what he could do."

My skin was hot. Too hot. Sweat blossomed over my chest. It felt like there was ice in my skull. I hated that he was right.

More than that though, I didn't care. There was no way I was going to stay behind while he—*while my guys* —went to war.

"I'm coming," I told him, letting my walls down just enough for Azrael to see the depth of my conviction. "And I'd like to see you try to stop me."

10

*N*one of them dared follow me back to our shared room.

They stayed far away as I tore the sheets from the bed and smashed the mirror above the sink, unable to handle the reflection of my own rage. They didn't come to soothe me as I paced and roared, screaming into the pillows.

It wasn't until I'd calmed down and was able to survey the room, and my destruction of it, with fresh eyes that a knock came at the door.

I felt utterly spent and completely disgusted with myself for having allowed my emotions to get the better of me. I was better than that. I wasn't a teenager bloodying her knuckles on the orphanage walls anymore. I was stronger. I was smarter.

But the assholes had gotten to me. I trusted them. I respected them.

And this was how they repaid me?

I bashed the back of my skull against the wall, sitting as I was with my knees bent on the floor, twirling Slashley between my fingers, I was hardly ready for civil conversation.

"Get fucked," I called, but my voice didn't carry any weight and the door swept open a moment later, revealing Azrael, outlined in the fluorescent lighting from the hall.

I laughed darkly to myself. "Ha. Smart fuckers. Sending the one that can't be killed."

"I assure you, I can be killed, however your ability to carry out the task is doubtful."

"Fuck you."

I caught a smirk on his lips before he was able to school his features, and the bastard stepped into the room despite my protests.

"What do you want, Azrael?"

He lifted a brow.

"For you to see reason..." he trailed off. "But it seems that was asking too much."

I gritted my teeth, the sound audible in the space between us as he sauntered nearer, closing the distance.

"So, we've changed tactics."

"We?"

"Your...harem, and myself."

This time I didn't correct him. I mean, it wasn't like he was wrong no matter which way you sliced it. I was theirs and they were mine, even when they were being incomprehensible dickwads.

I over-widened my eyes at him, wordlessly communicating for him to spit whatever he came here to say the fuck out before I lost my goddamned patience.

Azrael threaded his fingers behind his back, his gaze falling to rest on the angry set of my lips before speaking again.

"You're right. I have no doubt that we cannot stop you if you intend to join us. You've proven that by being able to break my brother's compulsion in New York."

"And?"

"And I'd rather enter this fight together, with our eyes open. Ready. Not divided."

"Gee thanks," I bit out. "It's not like I needed your *permission* but I'm oh so glad you've seen the light."

It didn't change the fact that they'd come up with this *plan* to leave me behind without my knowledge or my input. I expected some next level groveling if *any* of those fuckers wanted to make this shit right before the end of the week, and the battle to follow.

"They're already dividing several methods of *groveling* I think you'll find exceptionally acceptable."

A devious glint in his gaze made my belly flip and heat pool between my thighs despite my anger.

Damn my overacting fucking sex drive.

"There is *one* condition," Azrael spoke again before I

could redouble my efforts to tell him to get the fuck out of my room.

"A condition to what?"

"To our *allowing* you to come without a fight."

I squeezed the metal stake in my palm to keep from biting his head off.

"Oh really? And that is?"

Azrael bent and snatched the stake from my fingers before I could even register that he'd moved. He had the sharp tip of it pressed to the hollow dip just under my chin and his eyes were level with mine. Filled with fire. A challenge.

"We must ready your mind," he replied, and the huskily whispered words were almost lost with the thumping of my own pulse in my ears. "You've evolved leaps and bounds since your run in with my twin. And now, suddenly, you can block my ability to read you."

I threw up the wall I'd let falter as soon as he spoke the words, just because I could. And for the joy of seeing his smug look vanish. Though even frowning, there was still an edge of something else in his expression.

It looked almost like pride, and it made something I wasn't entirely used to swell beneath my breastbone.

"If you are to face my brother again, we want to ensure you can block any attempt to compel you. Or to read your moves before you can make them."

"I can," I affirm, though my tone lacks the confidence I feel. I have no idea how long the spell Amala placed over me will last. Without it I *was* able to break Rafe's compulsion, but that took blood, sweat, tears, and several *hours* to accomplish.

"You *broke* his compulsion," Azrael pressed. "But could you stop it altogether?"

He seems doubtful and it makes me want to test the theory almost as much as he clearly wants to.

I already knew Az would want to resume our mental training, so his request isn't a surprise. In fact, I *want* to practice on him more before we do this. What has my teeth still grating is the fact that he's framing it as a condition for my being able to go with them when we both fucking know that nothing would be able to stop me.

He's just trying to piss you off, I told myself, knowing it was true. What would piss him off would be to make it seem like he's *not* getting to you. Like he doesn't have any effect whatsoever.

That was what he wanted wasn't it? To get a rise out of me?

He wasn't going to get it.

Squaring my shoulders and in one swift movement, snatching the stake back from him and pressing it to *his* throat, Azrael's eyes revealed shock at the abrupt change of playing field. I grinned.

"When do we start?"

His smile was so wide it showed teeth. "Now."

I withdrew the stake from his throat and sheathed it, rising back to my feet. My gaze swept the floor, in search of my cellphone amid all the mess I'd created. "Food first," I decided. "Then I'm going to compel *you.*"

AZRAEL WATCHED me like a fucking serpent eyeing its next meal as tidied away the mess I'd made and swept up the broken glass from the bathroom floor after I'd eaten a dinner of barely warm pizza and wings.

He seemed intent on seeing that I followed through with my promise to train with him and he clearly had nothing better to do. I got the feeling he also knew the sort of effect he had on me. Not just his proximity, but the feel of eyes as he lazily watched me from the chair he lounged over in the corner of the room. One leg draped over the armrest; his chin propped up on two knuckles.

And hot damn if he didn't look like a fucking deity doing it.

On a whim, I decided if it was my *mind* to be trained tonight there was no reason for training leathers and dug out a pair of sweats and a tank top to wear instead.

"You want to turn around?" I asked Azrael, popping a hip.

He licked his lips, his eyelids drooping lower over his eyes. "Is that a rhetorical question?"

Fine.

I stripped down to my panties and changed, heart thrumming as Azrael's stare turned from watchful to downright liquid lust, and eventually, as he remembered I was off limits, to something much less excited. More...spiteful.

It suited him better.

I flicked my hair back over my shoulder and took my time lowering myself in front of him until I was seated cross-legged on the floor near his feet like a good little bitch. I cocked my head at him, fully aware that this tank without a bra made my boobs look like Christmas fucking morning.

It seemed even ancient men weren't immune to their charm.

"*Temptress*," he groaned, the word a slur on his lips, but the way his fingers dug into the armrest made me downright giddy.

"*Psycho*," I lobbied back with an innocent smile and shrugged. "We doing this or what?"

Immediately, I felt his presence in my thoughts. Like a foreign substance injected into the tight space of my skull. I pushed back against him, sweat beading over my chest. Fingers clawing into the floor.

He'd only been probing before. That was why it had seemed so easy to keep him out. This was full power. I could tell. And my face pinched at the difficulty of kicking his ass back out of my head.

"Shall I ease up?" he asked with a devilish half-smirk that made me want to punch his stupid face.

The anger was exactly what I needed to strengthen what I'd already naturally begun to form. The brick wall concealing my thoughts from Azrael didn't need to be placed brick by back-breaking brick. Not this time.

It *snapped* into place. One second not there.

The next second…

Azrael's brows furrowed.

I was really starting to like this little magic trick. *Thank you, Amala.*

"Shall I ease up?" I turned his own words back on him and checking to ensure the wall was securely in place, sealed of all cracks, I began my own assault.

Horror crossed Az's features for a brief second before he went to work building walls of his own.

I felt his mind in the distance. When I closed my eyes, I pictured it like a door in an infinite black space. A door of solid wood and iron. It mocked me with its strength. I grunted, exerting myself to the breaking point just to get nearer to it. Reaching out, my fingertips were still leagues away from pounding on that door.

My pulse picked up and in the dark infinity, it sounded like the drums of war.

I could do this.

It was like wading through quicksand, but inch by inch, I drew nearer. And in the dark I could sense Azrael. Feel his ability to keep me away waning. Distantly, I could hear his grunts of displeasure.

They propelled me onward until when I reached out again, the sharpened tips of my nails scraped ancient wood, tapped against cold iron. In a way, it was like touching Azrael himself. A very intimate part of him. Like the wood and iron were the barriers to his soul.

I made contact for barely a second before I was thrown out. I hissed through clenched teeth as I fell back, catching myself with my arms before I could be thrown back in the flesh, too.

Blinking through a bleary haze I found Azrael glaring down at me from his armchair, a muscle in his jaw jumping.

"Too close for comfort?" I asked, cocking my head.

He steeled himself and sat back in the chair once again.

"Amala gave you a strengthening charm, didn't she?"

I pursed my lips, neither confirming nor denying.

"It will wear off eventually..." he trailed off.

"I know. But for now—"

"It will be very useful. I'll have to remember to thank her the next time I see her. Before I rip her head from her shoulders."

My lips fell apart. "She's on our side," I argued, confused. "If you didn't believe that we wouldn't still be here."

Amala made no secret of knowing exactly where we were. If Az still thought she meant us harm, he'd have had us all out of here faster than I could blink.

"That doesn't change the fact that she was the

reason you were taken from me in the first place," he bit back, hands balling. "The things you endured at the hands of my brother...they cannot be undone. For that she will pay with her life."

I mean, he did have a point.

"Come now. Try again," Azrael pressed, lowering a hand to me.

"When you're learning, it's easier if there's contact. Take my hand."

I slid my hand into his, and his long fingers curled around my palm, making a small shudder course through me.

"I don't think I'll ever tire of that," he muttered, barely discernible.

"What?"

Azrael shook his head, his lips twitching up at one side. "Nothing."

He tested my defenses once again. At first with a gentle press against my brick wall. And then with a fucking sledgehammer. It rattled, but with a mega amount of effort, it held strong.

"Good," he said after a moment. "Now I seem to remember you saying you were going to *compel me*."

A challenge glimmered in his eyes and I jumped at the bait, feeling the flood of power that I knew would be dilating my pupils rising to the surface as I locked eyes with him. I backed my compulsion with everything I had. Drawing up from within. Every muscle taut.

"Punch yourself in the face."

The hand on his thigh twitched, jumping up from his lap a full two inches before it stilled.

My eyes widened.

"Oh my god," I breathed, unable to conceal my shock.

"Punch yourself in the face!" I tried again, throwing myself into the command, rocking up onto my knees to get closer to him. Never breaking eye contact.

His fingers twitched again and his hand trembled, but it didn't budge.

Fuck.

His lips pressed into a firm line and his brows drew low as he worked to deny my order.

Wait, I had an idea.

"Make me angry," I implored him, and his face screwed up in question.

"Just do it."

"You can't do this, Rose. You aren't strong enough."

"Is that all you got?"

He seemed to think about it for a second before speaking again. "The guys and I agreed that we should lock you up before we leave. Bind you in chains and leave a stack of pizzas and some water. Like leaving a mutt—"

Liquid fire injected into my veins and I roared. "Punch yourself in your stupid fucking face, Azrael."

His hand curled into a fist and turned on himself, moving faster than I could properly see. He stopped it.

Just a few inches before making contact and the loss was enough to make me lose my focus. I sighed heavily, slumping. Suddenly more exhausted than I'd been in weeks.

"That was incredible," Azrael said, drawing my focus back to him. "Impossible, actually. It *should* have been impossible."

He leaned forward, catching my chin between his thumb and forefinger. "You'd have made a fearsome immortal," he told me, emotion leaking into the statement. Reverence in his gaze.

Something inside of me ached at his words and I shivered, pulling back from his touch.

"What is it?"

I shook my head, pushing myself to standing. "Just worried I won't be strong enough," I lied. It was true that I may not be, but I wasn't exactly worried about it. I'd already decided a long time ago that if I lost my life to win this fight, it would be worth it.

"Then let's get back to work," Azrael offered. "I can say more cruel things if you'd like. I have plenty of ideas."

I smirked, reaching to take a long drink of my bottled water before sitting back down on the floor in front of him.

"Let's hear them. Lay it on me, asshole."

11

I muttered to myself as I went off in search of the guys. I hadn't succeeded in being able to do everything I'd wanted to be able to do. The things I thought I'd be able to do with Amala's help.

Azrael had been able to stop my compulsion every damned time. As much as I'd have loved to watch him pummel himself into the dirt, that wasn't what it was about. If I couldn't compel him, then I had no hope in hell of compelling Rafe. Which, if I was honest, I was sort of hoping I'd be able to do.

Daydreams of compelling him to castrate himself had filled my mind the whole way back from town.

It didn't seem like that was a possibility, *but* I had managed to block Azrael's compulsion which was a major fucking win.

It took countless attempts, and literally felt like my

brain was bleeding by the end, but I was able to *not* say the words he repeatedly demanded from my lips.

I want you.

The fucking self-righteous prick.

I shook my head as I walked, fuming, but at the same time so sexually frustrated I was sure there was actual steam lifting from the surface of my skin. I couldn't lie to myself. I was so damn sour about it because I *did* want him. And he knew that.

Which was why he forced me to say it over and over again.

I'd told him to make me mad, that my anger acted as a magnifier to my power, and he'd done just that. Knowing full well that forcing me to repeat those three words would drive me absolutely batty.

And it worked.

I got so riled up that in the end I was finally able to defeat him.

And his face... the look of disappointment when my lips remained closed, my face beat red and my gaze hot enough to melt metal—it was worth it.

If I wasn't at the mental breaking point, I'd have kept going, but if he kept pushing my buttons, regardless of the fact that I asked him to, I was liable to try to stake the fucker.

Hell, I may have succeeded.

I swallowed hard before peering into the gym, surprised at the jolt of disappointment when I found it empty.

Where the hell were they?

I was ready for them to start groveling. Too tired to be angry at them anymore.

I'd ream them out, make them swear not to *ever* try to control me again, and then I'd let it go.

We couldn't afford to be divided going into this shit.

Literal war was on our doorstep whether we liked it or not.

Ready or not.

It was a chance to save countless mortal lives in one fell swoop.

To save the girls.

We had to be in it together.

I sighed, retracing my steps, and peeking into our shared bedroom before continuing on to the lab.

Both were empty and a tick of worry made a muscle beneath my eye twitch.

"Ethan," I called down the corridor.

"Blake?"

If they were anywhere at all inside the bunker, they'd have heard me. Vamp hearing and all that.

An icy sliver of dread lodged itself in my spine and I cursed myself for leaving my stakes in the bedroom. Hadn't I promised myself not to go *anywhere* without them ever again? *Idiot.*

I raced down the hall and retrieved them from the bedroom, fear burrowing into my chest like poison.

"Rose," the voice came from the doorway and I

whirled on Azrael, trying to reign in the frantic tremor making my hands shake as I squeezed the chunk of metal in my palm.

"They've gone out," he explained, a worried crease in his forehead.

"But the amulet…"

There was only one of them.

It dawned on me all of a sudden that there really wasn't any need for it. With Amala clearly not working against us, we still needed to be very careful not to be seen by anyone working for Rafe, but we didn't need to hide like rats anymore.

I could go outside.

I felt like an idiot for not thinking of it before.

"It isn't wise to leave the compound," Azrael called after me as I brushed passed him and speed-walked down the hall. "Stay on the grounds."

I was just so freaking happy to be going back outside that I didn't even balk at the commanding tone.

I'd happily stay on the grounds. Hell, I was going to fucking sleep on them. I wondered if I could fashion a hammock out of the sheets in the bedroom, but that was a task for later. Right now, I had one singular focus. Get my ass to some fresh air.

Breathe it in.

I practically tripped out the door in my haste, pulling the metal shutter closed with a loud *bang* behind me. I grinned up at the moon, unbothered by the chill of the evening air.

"Rose?"

"Fuck!"

I spun, stake raised, leg pushed back, and arms squared for an attack.

"Everything okay?"

Frost's white-blonde head came into view from the shadows first as he emerged from the shadows of the trees at the edge of the compound.

"*Christ* Frost. I thought you were gone into town?"

He shrugged. "Nah. Eth and Blake went to get you some shit."

So, they were ready to commence with the groveling. Good. That made this easier.

"And you? Why didn't you go with them?"

He walked up to me, eyeing me up and down with a wary, but keen eye.

My skin bristled, and the little flame still flickering inside of me grew as I wondered if he was checking me for any indication that I'd done more than *train* with Azrael.

Frost crossed his arms over his mammoth chest. The black t-shirt strained with the motion and the contrast in color annoyingly made him look down-right drool worthy. I was a sucker for arm veins, and Frost has plenty.

"I think you're being a fucking idiot," he said, no hint of apology in the words. His expression hard and impassive. "The guys thought it might be a good idea for me to stay behind. Talk shit through with you."

I grit my teeth.

"So, you're hiding outside like a coward instead?"

His nostrils flared.

"You don't get it," he growled. "We can't lose you."

"You don't get to—"

"The fucking *human race* can't lose you, Rose."

His words stung like a snap to the face.

"If Rafe gets a hold of you. If he finds some fucked up way to make little vampire babies and walk in the sunlight whenever the hell he wants, what do you think will happen then? What will happen to the people you've worked so hard all this time to protect?"

"What's the alternative?" I shouted back. "Let the three of you and Azrael go without me? You know I'm the strongest of you three. You *need* me in this fight."

"So fucking selfish."

I shoved him hard in the chest, making him fall back a step.

"What the fuck did you just say?"

"You heard me."

"This isn't about the fight," I called him out, getting in his face.

Frost knew how good of a fighter I was. He had never made any secret of wanting to keep me safe, but he'd also always trusted me to take care of my damn self. He *knew* that I was going to be a key piece in winning this war. They all knew it.

They just didn't like it because they all knew the lengths I would go to make sure that happened.

"This is about *him*, isn't it?" I jabbed a finger towards the closed door to our left. "You're still fucking pissy because of—"

"Drop it, Rose."

"*Admit it.*"

"Drop it."

I shoved him again. "Fuck you."

The muscles in Frost's jaw tightened and I turned away before either one of us said something we'd regret. Guilt tugged at my chest as I stomped through the gravel toward the trees. When I'd gotten into this with my guys, I'd never imagined even wanting to add anyone else, especially not Azrael.

Frost felt betrayed.

Maybe I did, too. Betrayed by my own fucking emotions.

But we needed to call this what it was and not pretend our frustration with each other was about anything else.

"Where are you going?"

Frost's voice had a hard edge to it that made me grit my teeth on a snarky response.

"Away from you."

"Yeah, go ahead, Rose. Walking away from a problem always solves it."

"Says the guy who *never* wants to talk about shit."

"At least I was honest about my shit. You need to own yours."

I spun on my heel and threw my hands up. "What

ELENA LAWSON

was I thinking? Arguing with you is clearly the better solution!"

Frost met my furious gaze with one to rival it. We stared at one another like that for several heartbeats. Breaths clouding the air around our faces.

My insides squeezed as his expression changed. As his gaze left my eyes, straying lower.

Apparently, we were going for option number three.

He came at me like the wind, crushing my lips to his as he tackled me to the ground. We fetched up hard against a tree and I shoved him off, sending him reeling into another one.

I pounced at him and ripped his shirt apart, my nails leaving score marks across his chest. He growled and I echoed the sound. Our mouths crashed together, tongues warring for dominance. That was the language we spoke, that vicious battle, the fight for power.

That was how one of us would have to make our point.

Frost's belt whipped off into the darkness and I yanked hard on his short, white-blonde hair. He instinctively tilted his head to the side, and I had the sudden urge to bite down. I wanted to see him blissed out by my own power the way I'd seen him under Blake's. Wanted him to succumb to it. To beg for it.

I blinked and the moment was gone, taking my breath with it. Frost spun us around in my distraction, ripping yet another one of my shirts and pressing my bare breasts against the rough bark. My pants had come undone at some point and now hung around my knees. He leaned in close, his breath whispering across my skin. I shuddered, both pissed that he'd gotten the upper hand and yet so fucking wet for him.

He slid his hands around my hips and down between my legs, fingers stroking my slick folds. A gasp got stuck in my throat as I resisted the impulse to react. It took everything I had not to open my legs for him and give in. I wanted him but, guilt be damned, I wouldn't capitulate on this one.

I needed to prove my resolve as much as he did.

"Is this for me, or for him?" he hissed in my ear.

Oh, that was the wrong fucking thing to say.

I threw my head back into his jaw. He flinched back enough to release me, and I kicked my pants away, now naked to the stars. I didn't give a shit who saw me.

Frost came at me again and I swept his legs out from under him. He landed hard on his back, but I was on him before he could recover. Vampire or not, he was no match for me. I sat on his chest with my knees pinning his arms down, my pussy inches from his face, and watched his icy blue eyes lock onto it and glaze over with lust.

"It's for whoever I damn well want to give it to," I growled. "Do you think you deserve it?"

I stroked myself right in front of him, on top of him, using his love of watching against him. His muscles strained under my knees, but he didn't try to break free, and his eyes were focused on my fingers. Leaning back into the moonlight, I gave him a better view.

The combination of being outside, of being the dominant force, of forcing him to watch me masturbate, brought the dragon roaring to the surface. My fingers pumped faster, heat unspooling from my core. A whimper escaped me when I saw the hunger in his stare. Frost licked his lips and I suddenly wanted those lips, that tongue, to go to work for me.

"Do you want it?"

His eyes darted to mine and, though his jaw muscles rippled as he clenched his teeth, he gave the barest nod. I kept going, fingers sliding back and forth, and his arms jerked, trying to break free. A quickening sensation burned deep inside and I moaned softly. My hips jerked as I circled the nub of my clit, which made Frost fight harder against me.

I loved my guys taking control in the bedroom, but the kind of seductive power running through me now was addictive. He knew I would cum whether he helped me or not. It was his choice to participate, but even if he didn't, he'd be forced to watch.

Damn, it was hot.

Then my knees hit the ground and Frost's hands grabbed my ass, pushing me into his face. I pitched forward, catching myself on my hands as his mouth covered my sex. He massaged my cheeks roughly, his hot tongue tying me into knots. My chest tightened as he pushed me toward the edge, anticipating the fall.

He flattened his tongue, lapping at the juices I'd stirred up. I clenched my fists, ripping handfuls of grass from the ground as I bucked against his attention. His tongue flicked back and forth, alternating fast and slow to drive me crazy.

When his fingers entered me, pumping me hard from the start, I was lost to the euphoric riptide. It crashed over me, pulling me under so I couldn't tell which way was up, my breath lost in the waves.

Frost's warm hands grabbed my hips, and I hadn't realized he'd gotten up until I felt his cock pressing against my entrance. I was so wet that he met no resistance and I slammed back against him with a gasp. My insides hadn't let go of the first orgasm yet, but the next was building on top of it with each thrust.

But a moment of clarity reminded me that he'd just taken control, and I couldn't have that right now.

There was a fight I had to win.

Much as I hated to, I broke away, spinning on my knees to knock him to his back again. He rolled to his feet before I could pin him down, so I ran at him and leapt. I registered confusion in his eyes a half-second before he caught me, then I tugged his head back to look at me.

"Fuck me like you mean it."

I sucked his bottom lip between my teeth, biting hard without drawing blood, my tongue lashing out to soothe it. He pressed me back against a tree, adjusting his grip on my hips to enter me again. I drove my hips in time with his brutal thrusts, and I suspected I'd have more than a couple bruises when this was over.

"You couldn't just be content with the three of us, could you?" he panted.

Is that what he thought it was about? That I wasn't happy with them? "More content than you are that my emotions don't revolve solely around you, apparently."

Frost growled again and pressed his forehead to mine, his pace slowing. "Dammit, Rose. This isn't just about me."

"Oh yeah? If it's not about you, then why are you the only one getting butt-hurt about it?"

I wrapped myself around him tighter and flung my weight to the side, taking us down again. We rolled and I landed on top, pinning his shoulders down even as he thrust into me from underneath. I met him blow for blow, thighs burning through the exertion but determined to take what was mine. Fire licked my insides, my senses coming alive as I fucked him, loved him, punished him.

Frost cursed under his breath and gave in. I saw the moment when he submitted, throwing his head back and closing his eyes. My fingernails dug into his chest, bracing myself for the rush of pleasure his cock promised.

Guilt-tinged victory was mine.

"Frost." His eyes snapped open again and I had to

concentrate on my words before I exploded. "I'm still yours, too. Now cum with me."

His lips parted and I took them before he could speak. He grunted, thrusts becoming frantic as we rushed forward together. Only the sounds of the outdoors and slapping of flesh surrounded us. My passage convulsed around him as another orgasm surged through me. I cried out in time with Frost as he followed me, his steel length flooding me with heat.

Seeing stars became a literal phrase that night, and I felt like I'd float off into the sky with them. Only Frost's arms kept me earth-bound. He was my rock.

No matter what else happened, he was still my Frost.

"Why are you so goddamned stubborn?"

I shuddered, easing back on him. My sharp finger-nails skimmed lightly over his scalp and his eyelids fluttered. "Because I know what I want, I'll do what it takes to have it, and I'll sacrifice to protect it. Just like you would."

"Would you sacrifice me to have him?" he asked.

Ouch. That stung.

"That's like asking if I'd chop off my arm." I cupped his face and stared into his beautiful eyes. "I don't think I could do any of this without all of you by my side. You're all unique and mean something different to me, but you're all equally important."

Frost sighed and pressed his lips to mine in the gentlest kiss he'd ever given me. Warmth filled my

ELENA LAWSON

chest, something that felt like his acceptance or acknowledgment. His hands smoothed up my thighs, squeezing lightly.

He glanced away. "Take him, if that's what you really want."

"I don't like being told how to live or what to do," I said. "But I also know I don't want to hurt you."

Shaking his head, he huffed a laugh, his cheeks turning pink. "Truth is, maybe I didn't want to admit my feelings either. I hated him for how he came into our lives, but he's hot as fuck. He's got this...I don't know...he's got something going on. So, I guess I'm saying I get it. You know I'm not good at those kinds of words, so I—"

I cut him off with my fingers against his soft lips. In all my years, I'd never seen Frost so vulnerable. It both broke my heart and filled it full to bursting. He fucking wanted Azrael, too. He just didn't want to admit it to himself. I was willing to bet it had been hard enough for him to accept the sexual bond between him, Ethan, and Blake. Accepting that he also had those feelings for Az would have been confusing. He would have denied them just like I denied them at first, too.

Finally, I understood his reluctance. I understood it more than he could ever realize.

I didn't know what I would've done if he'd continued to protest, but I did know one thing.

I fucking loved this man.

"*I* see you two worked your shit out," Blake said, pulling me from a half-asleep daze. My heavy head lifted from Frost's shoulder and I found him and Ethan through slitted eyes.

They walked up the gravel drive and to where Frost and I sat, him propped up against the trunk of a wide oak tree, and me propped up against him.

I couldn't tell how long we'd been sitting like that, in a state of undress. Our clothes in torn tatters scattered around. Illustrating the blast radius of our hate fuck session.

A small grin tugged at the corner of my mouth and my inner thighs squeezed at the freshness of the memory.

Ethan knelt in front of us, a plastic bag held open between his hands. "All of your favorites," he told me with a hesitant smile. "Cheetos—the family size bag.

Gatorade—the blue one. And all the jerky and instant coffee a girl could ask for."

My heart ached a little in my chest as I reached out, drawing the Cheetos from the bag, and tearing into it with sloppy sleep-addled fingers.

I opened my mouth to give them the reaming I promised but found I lacked the energy.

Instead, lamely, I muttered, "Don't be dicks."

"We were total *total* dicks," Ethan agreed.

"The biggest," Blake added.

"Forgive us?" Frost crooned, pushing his face into my neck. His warm breath caressed the sensitive skin there, making me shudder.

I moaned a little, stuffing two Cheetos into my face.

"Fine," I said, pulling away. "Forgiven."

Ethan high-fived Blake and they all shared a conspiratorial grin.

"But if you *ever* pull some shit like that again I am going to dick punch each of you. *Hard.*"

Blake paled.

"*And,*" I added, eyeing them all in turn. "I'll withhold sex. For, like, a really long time."

Blake let loose a short laugh at that, lifting a hand to rub the back of his head.

"Okay so maybe I won't withhold sex."

"Nah," Frost agreed. "You can't say no to us."

Bastards.

A yawn took me between Cheetos and my eyes burned. Frost tugged me in closer, lending me some more of his body warmth. His relaxed muscles making the best pillow.

"We should get you back inside," Ethan said, moving into position to lift me up from the ground. I gently pushed his extended hands away, shaking my head.

"No," I moaned, ditching the Cheetos, and curling up on the ground, using my arm as a pillow as I yawned again. "I think I'll just sleep out here from now on. Fuck that dungeon."

Ethan pushed the hair out of my face. "It'll get cold," he argued.

"Our queen can't have dirt for a pillow," Blake barked. "Shit ain't right."

He vanished a second later and I had to agree. My bare arm and the side of my tit was starting to itch from the scratchy pine, rock, and leaf covered ground. I rolled, trying to brush it off before my body was jerked swiftly upward, causing a startled gasp to tumble from my lips.

Upside down on Frost's shoulder, my brain had trouble making sense of the massive shape blocking most of Blake from view. At least until he dropped it onto the ground, causing a mushroom cloud of dirt.

The mattress from our bed in the bunker laid beneath the sparse tree canopy. Under the stars. Atop it, he dropped an armful of pillows and blankets before Frost tossed me down atop it all.

It was Ethan who helped set it all right. Gently nudging me so he could get a pillow under my head and cover my half naked body with the thick comforter.

I burrowed into it all, shivering with warm and comfort. Breathing the fresh air deeply.

"Will you stay?" I whispered. "Until the sun comes up?"

The mattress dipped in all directions as the three of them piled in. Arms wrapping around my middle and around my legs. The comfort and warmth were almost enough to send me shooting over the edge of oblivion into sleep, but...

"I love you," I muttered before feeling my eyes drift fully closed.

I could have already been sleeping, but whether real or imagined they each replied;

"Always."

"Love the shit out of you, Rosie."

And Blake, without words, but the squeeze of his fingers around my ribcage and the way he pressed his face into my back was enough for me to know. He loved me too.

"MORNING, SUNSHINE," Blake's husky voice whispered against my cheek and I moaned into the pillow. Truth be told, I'd been teetering on the edge of waking for a while, but I just wasn't ready to pull the trigger. I was too cozy. The air was too clean and fresh.

I could've stayed there forever.

Wait…

I jolted up, realizing the warmth I felt on the back of my head was sunlight. Eyes still coated in a sheen of sleep, I rubbed them forcefully and squinted up at Blake. "What are you still doing out here? The sun—"

"Relax," he cooed, patting me on the head with a mischievous grin. "I took my vitamins."

I sat up straighter, trying to force my eyes to stop burning and grimacing when sheer force of will didn't work.

"We didn't want to leave you alone up here. Unprotected."

"You could've—"

"You needed to sleep," he argued.

"Yeah, but we need all the elixir—"

"Would you shut up."

Blake tugged me back down to laying, pulling me atop his chest. "I figure I have about fifteen or twenty more minutes to enjoy this before I have to drag both our asses back down to the pit of despair. Let me enjoy it?"

I resisted the urge to argue some more and did my best to relax into the crook of his arm, sighing.

"This is how it should've been," Blake said after a time, his voice low and distant as though he were a million miles away.

"Hmm?"

He squeezed me tighter to his body and I gratefully

snuggled my cold nose into his bare tatted chest. "This," he repeated.

I propped myself up on an elbow to see his expression, finding it somber. His dark eyes somehow darker now even though they were drenched in natural sunlight.

"Mornings in the sun," He explained with a sad smile. "Drawing lazy circles on your skin as you sleep."

"And then what?" I asked, seeing where he was going and needing to put an end to the train of thought before he let it run away with him. I'd been down that road before.

The *what if* intersection.

Where *if only* and *should've been* cross ways.

But you don't get to go down either of those roads. Not in this life. Not how we live.

His dark brows drew in, confused.

"Get married?" I asked, my tone mocking even though I was trying hard to keep it under control. "Pop out a couple of kids and live in the suburbs?"

His gaze flitted away, glancing down at the dirt.

"Can you picture me in that sort of life, Blake? With an apron and a whisk? Rushing little Rosie and Blake Jr. out the door to soccer?"

I barked a laugh at the image.

"You can't think like that," I continued. "I don't. I'm not built for that life. Hell, I don't *want* it. I don't think you do, either…"

It took him a minute, but when Blake finally

dragged his gaze back to mine, the dark vulnerability I'd seen there in his stare was all but gone, replaced with the cool mask he always wore. "No," he breathed. "Maybe not the white-picket fence or the kid...but I mean I could see myself jamming out to rock radio in a nice minivan, couldn't you?"

I burst out laughing at that, punching him in the arm.

"What brought this on?"

He shrugged.

"You're like an angel when you sleep, you know that?"

"With my eyes half open and drool pooling on my pillow?"

He shook his head.

"I almost hoped it wasn't you, you know? When we figured out you were The Black Rose. I hoped we couldn't find you because you found a better life. With a husband and a nice house. I hoped you were happy somewhere."

I cocked my head at him.

"You deserve better than a life filled with danger. With death."

"That sounds boring as fuck."

He levelled me with a knowing gaze.

"Okay, it might be nice not to be hunted by half the vampire population—"

"More like 75 percent."

"Semantics," I muttered. "In a few days, the biggest

part of our problem will be dead. Once that happens whatever remains of his followers will scatter like the roaches they are."

"And then what?"

"And then…" I think, trying to explain what I hope will happen, no matter the odds stacked against us. "I don't know. We make sure the vampires stay in line. We kill whoever doesn't. We protect the mortals."

"Forever?"

I bit my lower lip and glanced away, a knife in my gut. "Until I can't anymore."

"What do you—"

Blake hissed and I snapped my head up, finding his face contorted in pain. A wisp of smoke lifted from his chest and he disentangled himself from the blankets, rushing in a blur of speed to the bunker, where he wrenched open the door and vanished into the dark.

"Get inside," he called back to me, the demand tainted with the sound of his discomfort.

And just like that, the spell was broken.

Return to normal life in 3...2...

"Rose!"

"I'm coming!" I hollered back, cursing to myself as I tied a scrap of Frost's shirt across my boobs like a bandeau. The picture of chastity.

*O*ne last run.

Blake and Frost would hit up the blood bank in the nearest city, getting enough to sate and strengthen our entire army before the fight to come.

Days. That was all that remained now.

We couldn't afford to wait much longer. Keeping the recruits fed and in line was a constant battle. We'd already lost nearly twenty to squabbles among themselves. Bodies were carted out and buried in the woods daily now.

If it kept up, they'd all be dead before we could even do what we set out to.

"Why can't I go again?" I asked, itching to lose my shit.

Honestly? I was damn proud of myself for how I was keeping my head lately. It'd been weeks and I hadn't murdered anyone. Okay, well there was that one vampire dude, but he attacked first. Not my fault.

"If you're going to lead these vampires into a new era don't you think you should get to know them?" Ethan asked.

"I don't really see the point," Frost argued.

"That's not what it's about anyway," Blake injected. "It's like Az said. You need more practice and there's a line-up of volunteer vamps waiting to do whatever the fuck you ask them to."

I groaned, shoving away my half-eaten veggie burger. Frost ordered it by mistake. Either that or he was trying to kill me.

The thing tasted like too much cumin and had a texture like sawdust.

"We'll be back before you know it," Frost winked, folding one duffel bag into another, and slinging them over his shoulder.

"You're ready to leave then?" Azrael said, appearing in the doorway like a specter. Honestly? I was starting to get used to it.

Frost stiffened but replied with an easy tone. "Yeah. heading out now. We'll be back long before sun-up."

My blue-eyed vamp glanced uneasily between Az and I before dipping past the ancient vamp and into the hall. "Let's go," he said, shooting heated stares in Blake's direction, and warning ones in Ethan's.

Curiosity piqued, I squinted at the trio.

Unaware I was doing it, Frost's thoughts filtered

out like a spool gently tugged at first, and then ripped free to be left unspooling all over the floor.

I need to get out of here before I fucking lose it...

And Ethan needs all the time he can to get the—

The thought was cut short with a *nope* and Frost gaze flicked to mine, his eyes narrowing.

"Are you in my head?" he demanded; lips pressed in a hard line. Abruptly, because I wasn't ready for it, he managed to shove me out and I sputtered, cheeks heating.

"Sorry," I muttered. "I didn't even realize..."

"I'm not in your head messing around with your private shit," he hissed, and guilt ravaged my chest at the slap of his words before he reined himself in. "Fuck. Sorry. I'm just...a little on edge, you know?"

I nodded, but the suspicion was still there. There was clearly something he didn't want me to know and it bothered me that he would hide something from me.

Not just him, though, I realized with a start as Blake finished tucking the tails of his laces into his shoes and stood, and Ethan bit the inside of his cheek as he cleared off his lab table. None of them were looking at me.

Frost just bit my head off and neither jumped to my defense.

What the fuck was going on here?

I had the heart to feel at least a little guilty about it when I prodded against the walls of Ethan's mind, only

ELENA LAWSON

to meet resistance. Iron-clad resistance that savored of the same sort Azrael used.

If I pressed hard enough, I knew I could break through. None of them were even a fraction as strong as Azrael was, but that was beside the point. I wouldn't force my way into their minds.

I cut Az a withering stare and he had the decency to glance away as Blake strode past him to join Frost in the hall.

When their footfalls began to dissipate and I heard the metal curtain of the door crash shut behind them from afar, I turned on Az. "What's going on?"

"I'm sure I don't know what you mean."

Fine. He wouldn't tell me, but there was one guy in here who would spill when pressed. Ethan wouldn't lie to me.

"Do *you* want to tell me what's going on?"

A micro-tightening around his lips was the only indication that I'd made him uncomfortable as he shrugged. "Azrael has been giving us a few lessons too."

It wasn't a lie, but I knew Ethan. He wouldn't meet my gaze. It wasn't a lie, but it wasn't the truth, either.

"*Ethan.*"

"Rose, just let it go."

"Come," Azrael beckoned, stretching out a hand to me. "Shall we go and check in on our recruits?"

My teeth ground together audibly as I pulled away from Ethan and turned to stalk past Az, pushing his proffered hand from my path.

I wouldn't force Ethan to tell me. Knew he wouldn't in front of Azrael. I needed to speak to him alone. Then he would see that whatever he thought he was better off not sharing wasn't worth it.

He would see that keeping something from me right now, standing on the edge of battle, was a bad fucking idea.

"Are you coming?" I hissed back at Azrael and double checked all my weapons were where they should be as we made our way to the main barracks.

"Rose!" Valentina exclaimed as we entered and I almost choked on a cloud of sex-scented air, finding her ass naked astride one of her vampire men, with a different cock levelled at her mouth.

The males looked anything but apologetic as Valentina jumped off the impressive length beneath her and snatched up a shawl to wrap around her shoulders.

"Don't stop on my account," I said with a laugh, some of the ire leaving my muscles and mind. "But maybe keep it contained to one of the rooms? You know, instead of the main hallway."

It was clear they'd somehow spilled out. The majority of the other doors in the hall were shut, but the one directly next to them, leaned at an odd angle, hanging ajar. They'd obviously crashed into somehow and landed out here.

I was fucking impressed.

"What are you doing here?"

"Kissing babies," I joked. "Shaking hands. The usual."

She tipped her head to one side and I remembered the language barrier. Her English was impeccable, but some things would be lost on her.

"We're just checking in," I explained, gesturing to Azrael at my back.

Valentina dipped her head to him in something like a bow and I had to stifle a laugh at the silly formality. It wasn't the fucking dark ages. Was bowing really necessary?

"We've come to tell you and the others that we'll be leaving the day after next, just before dawn. And that a new blood supply will be delivered this eve," Azrael told her.

"I'll spread the word."

"There," I trilled, turning back to Az. "No need to see the rest of them. Valentina will pass on the news. Let's go."

"Not so fast," he chided, catching me around the elbow before I could rush back the way we'd come.

I groaned.

"I need to test loyalties," he whispered against my ear, causing me to still. "One last time before we depart. If there is any doubt I would prefer to know now."

But he didn't just want to know. He left the other

bit unspoken. If there was any doubt—he intended to be rid of it. Which meant there could be some action.

Alright. My interest was piqued.

Unconsciously, my fingertips found the cool, smooth planes of Slayla and Stabitha between my thighs.

Azrael gave me a nod and I watched his adams apple bob in his throat.

He liked me like this, I realized.

Murderous. Teetering on the brink of sanity.

Noted.

Something low in my belly clenched as I was suddenly reminded of my tryst with Frost outside the other night. He'd given me permission.

I was three for three.

I could have Azrael if I wanted him.

My throat went dry and I coughed, swallowing down hard to wet it again before looking away.

Just because I *could,* didn't mean I had to.

"Right," I squeaked awkwardly, inwardly bitch-slapping myself back to the present. "Well then let's go. We should let Val get back to…"

Valentina tucked her long hair back from her face, shooting coy glances at her unapologetically naked, and still *very hard* mates.

One of them, the really pretty one with the dark eyes and light hair, scooped her up in his arms and rushed back into the bedroom with the others in tow. The last one to enter managed to get the door somewhat closed, leaning it against the frame in a way that would do absolutely nothing to block the sound, but would at least help to block the view.

Not that any of them seemed to mind being watched.

It dawned on me as the door began to open and the vampires emerged from their rooms in various states of wakefulness, that Valentina was one of only two females among our ranks. The other, a quiet woman with sinful curves and a beautiful mane of black curls stuck mostly to herself and her small group of only three mates.

I'd seen her only once before, on a monitor, and she was even more magnificent in person. Her deep brown eyes piercing. She was the sort who made you wonder if you might die just by being in her airspace.

I admired her for it.

She bowed her head as she approached with her three mates behind her, several others coming to pay their respect behind them.

The bow wasn't odd, what *was* odd was how it was directed at *me* instead of Azrael.

I swallowed a laugh and lifted my chin.

"We've come with news," Azrael said, launching into a short explanation of how the departure would work and that everyone must follow his instructions or risk exposure and certain death.

He was a natural leader.

Focused. Unyielding. Fair. Slightly terrifying.

I found myself watching him as he spoke, my insides tightening and toes curling.

It was...kind of hot watching him be all master-y.

I wondered how he'd master me.

"Rose?" Azrael prodded and I realized it wasn't the first time he's said my name.

"What?"

"Is there anything you'd like to add?"

I blinked, eyes darting between Az and the ever-growing gathering of vamps now clogging the hallway of the main barracks.

He was stalling for time. That telltale line was there between his brows. He was reading them, checking for dissent among the ranks.

Think, Rose. Say something.

"Um..."

"When this is over," a male vampire said, stepping forward around the vampire woman, giving her and her mates as wide a berth as he could. "I'll follow you wherever you go."

The vampire was tall, with a sexy flop of dark hair dipping down to cover one eye and killer face structure. Like, it should be illegal to have that symmetrical of a face. That strong of a jaw combined with those high cheekbones.

Pretty, but in a dangerous way.

If I wasn't already tied to three—scratch that—*four* vampires I might've swooned. But four was fucking plenty for me.

"What's your name?" I asked, unsure how to respond to declarations of loyalty, especially from a vampire who looked like he'd been around the block a few times. He may be on our side now, after I'd given him the sun, but I got the distinct feeling from him that he wasn't always that way.

"Draven, my queen."

"Uh...yeah. I'm not, like—"

"I'm with you as well," another called, followed by a chorus of others.

Azrael face hardened as he scanned the grouping, his gaze zeroing in on one particular vampire hovering near the back of the gathering.

It was hard, especially with all the shouting and bodies pressed tightly together, but I searched through the minds of the vampires, trying to pick up the voice of the one Azrael was keenly listening in on.

This was meant to be a practice run for me too after all.

I found it a heartbeat later. The voice I was looking for.

No. Don't think that.

Stop thinking.

Stop thinking!

Well, that was interesting.

I gave the vampire who called himself Draven a tight nod, quickly scanning his thoughts for doubt before moving past him. His thoughts were a dark and tangled web of guilt, but there was a glimmer of hopefulness. He thought that following me would redeem him.

I fucking doubted that, but I'd let him try. It was better than having another supernatural murderer on the loose.

Listening intently to the thoughts of those I passed, Azrael followed me as we carved a straight line through the vampires. My senses tingled with unease. That prickle on the back of my neck was practically buzzing. My blood thrumming in my veins.

Their thoughts rose and crashed like waves around me.

The last Vocari.

I can't believe we're following her, *but it's better than the alternative.*

Goddess.

I wonder what her pussy would feel like.

Her blood smells like honey.

Fuck, I'm so thirsty.

Control. Control. Control.

"You," I said, pointing at the one who's was actively trying to think of anything except for what his mind was trying desperately to work through. The vampire was clearly young. He had no idea how to conceal his thoughts and the vibe I got from him was of a weaker flavor. Barely an itch where Azrael's was a full-on attack at my back now that I was back in tune with that sixth sense.

"Will you follow us when this is all over?"

I popped a hip and cocked my head at him, listening in. "Y-yes. I will."

Fuck that, he thought and then immediately after. *No. No, I didn't mean that.*

His eyes flicked to Azrael. He clearly knew that Az could read his thoughts, but he seemed to be oblivious to the fact that I could as well. Good. Perhaps I'd keep that my little secret.

Letting my compulsion flood my voice, I locked in on him, holding his watery blue eyes captive with mine. "Tell me how you really feel."

He bared his teeth, gritting them hard against the words trying to escape his lips.

"Go on. Tell me."

"You'll pay for what you did," he spat in a rush, no longer able to block the words or his vicious thoughts from ringing clear and true.

You killed her. You fucking bitch. I'll fucking end you. First chance I get.

"Looks like you missed one," I muttered to Azrael and he stepped up next to me frowning down at the weasel of a vampire.

"You're right. It seems I have."

The vampire was practically vibrating. Frothing at the mouth. But I was holding him steady with pure will. I found it easy, in fact, and I shuddered a little at the realization that I didn't need to speak to force him not to move a muscle.

Testing a theory, I broke eye contact completely.

The vampire continued to sputter and hiss but did not move.

I grinned at Azrael and he gawked at me, clearly shocked. Maybe a little jealous even.

"Are you…"

"I think so," I replied. "Is this normal?"

"Not exactly."

Cool.

But I mean I wasn't going to hold the fucker still while I staked him. Where was the fun in that?

"Can I have a little space?"

The vampires in my immediate area dispersed, moving backward, whispering among themselves. Only Azrael remained.

I gave him a look.

"You're perfectly capable. I'm just here as ornamentation. Proceed."

I giggled a little at that.

"It's Doug, right?" I asked the vamp, drawing a stake to twirl it between my fingers.

He trembled.

"Well, Doug. I'm not sure what I did to piss you off but—"

"You killed her!" he shouted, and I added a silent command to shut the fuck up to the one already holding him in place.

His lips sealed.

Oh my fucking god if that wasn't the coolest shit ever.

My blood sang with exhilaration.

His thoughts shouted louder than he ever could have spoken, though. Not just words, but images.

His queen lying dead on the concrete, her mates bloodied bodies around her cold, lifeless form. He'd been returning from a hunt and had found his entire brood dead.

I understood how that must have pained him.

But I also saw how he missed torturing innocent humans with his queen. He missed the sounds of their sweet screams as he drained them lifeless. He liked the young ones. Boys. No more than thirteen.

Filth.

"Doug here seems to think it's okay to rape and kill innocent prepubescent boys. I just want to make this absolutely fucking clear," I shouted, my voice wavering with rage. "When we defeat Raphael, there *will* be a new order. You may feed. You may fuck. You can do whatever the hell you please. But you will *not* rape. You will *not* murder. You will not touch *a single hair on a child's head* ever. And you will erase every trace of your contact from the minds of those you feed on."

Even that wasn't enough. But it had to be. Otherwise, there would be no space in this world for them. For men like my guys. If they didn't deserve to live. Then how could I rationalize keeping my men from harm?

It was the only way.

"And if you do *not* abide by these rules, I will fucking gut you."

The whispers began again, and I listened closely to the barrage of new thoughts in the room. Some were sour over it, but most, it seemed, truly believed they could follow those rules. It gave me hope that there could be some form of truce—of peace—between men and monsters.

But for that to happen, we needed to *win*.

And we could show no mercy.

I released Doug from my hold and he nearly dropped to his face in his haste to rush me.

It was easy to dodge his attack, parrying to the left and clocking him in the head hard enough to crack his skull. Dazed, he didn't see me coming as I kicked him from behind, sending him flying to the ground. He rolled onto his back, clutching his head between his hands.

But that wasn't the head he needed to be protecting.

I stomped on his junk, grinding it to mincemeat under the heel of my boot to the soundtrack of his wheezing screams. I didn't ease up, holding my booted foot there firmly, preventing him from escape.

If he moved, he'd risk ripping what was left of his man bits clean off his body.

I was willing to bet it was agony.

I felt no remorse.

Tears stung his eyes as he wailed, body trembling. I

lifted my head from his pathetic form to meet the eyes of our army. Taking my time. Trying to meet each and every stare with fire.

They needed to know—to understand. Disobedience would not be tolerated.

A stab of worry made my impassioned stare falter for a second as I realized how fucked up it was that I should lead them. I wasn't a vampire. I was what they were born out of, sure. But I wasn't like them.

I'd never *be* like them.

I shook my head, fixating my rage back where it belonged.

"Bye, bye Dougie. Say hi to the devil for me, would ya?"

14

$\mathcal{I}$t was barely a two-hour flight to New York.
The final days leading up to our depar-
ture from the pits of despair beneath the Canadian soil
were a monotonous routine of eating, sleeping, and
training.

If you could call picking at congealed poutine
eating and waking every two hours sleep. Training was
about the only thing going as planned. After my fun
with Dougie in the barracks, Azrael hadn't let me
return to the lab. He'd dragged me outside for our daily
mental aerobics.

It made a world of difference—being outside.

Over the days, we took to training several hours
together in the night, under the stars.

I was distracted, trying to put it out of my head that
my guys were hiding something from me since they
each insisted, they weren't. But even distracted, by day

three—the day before we were to leave—*I compelled Azrael.*

He'd been positively red in the face trying to resist, but in the end, he'd done it. Muttering through gritted teeth, he decked himself in the face. Hard. I thought I heard something crack in there.

I felt bad...a little.

Nah.

Not really.

"Let's run through it again," Ethan said as the plane rolled to a stop. With the window covers all drawn it was impossible to tell where we were, but we had a timeline of events that needed to happen exactly as Azrael planned. So, I knew without needing to see that we were in a hangar.

I knew that the other plane, the one carrying the rest of the vampires, was already here, waiting for us.

We left as soon as the sun set.

Taking the route Azrael laid out for us.

Our vampire army was split into smaller groupings, made to take a total of fourteen different routes to the airstrip in the case that one grouping or more were intercepted or seen by anyone loyal to Raphael.

Leaving in broad daylight would have made departing, and arriving, much safer, but we needed to conserve all the elixir we could for the fight tomorrow.

Having the sun on our side was the only way we'd survive this.

Az's intel suggested that Rafe managed to add

another hundred to his ranks just in the last few days alone.

His force now outnumbered ours two to one.

It was imperative that we strike now, before he would be able to get any stronger than he already had.

"We load ourselves and the others into the vehicles," I started, mentally checking off the list as I went. "Each vehicle has a pre-planned route already plugged into the GPS. We take those routes and don't stop for anything. Once the route is memorized, it needs to be wiped from the car's memory."

"Right," Ethan nodded, tapping the screen of a tablet where he'd managed to hack into the city's traffic cameras. Something about the fact that he knew how to do that was just so fucking sexy. "I'll keep an eye on the building as we go and re-route anyone I need to if it looks like Rafe is sending out scouts."

The door to our private plane opened and an attendant poked his head inside. "You may depart," he stated in a distant voice. Azrael arrived here yesterday, alone, and had already taken care of compelling every mortal we'd come into contact with to do our bidding and then immediately forget that they ever dealt with us at all.

So long as we didn't divert from his plan at all, we'd make it to the hotel without incident.

Azrael booked out the entire building. Well, sort of.

He'd procured a list of current guest bookings and

contact information and compelled them to book elsewhere.

When we arrived, each small group of vampires would effectively *be* the missing guests arriving for check-in.

The only thing we couldn't help was arriving in the middle of the night. But that was why we had so many different vehicles and routes. And three different parking garage destinations that would allow for a mostly concealed trek to the underground elevators leading to the hotel lobby.

If any grouping was spotted or captured, they'd only need to withstand torture for mere hours before we attacked.

It was already midnight.

Sunrise was at 7:21am if Google was to be believed.

We had a little over seven hours until all hell broke loose in the streets of New York City.

Seven hours to get to our 'base', get hundreds of vampires tattooed—all three guys would be helping with that thanks to the crash course Ethan gave them last night, and tip off the authorities to our false bomb to get the streets cleared before going in.

It was going to be tight but waiting until tomorrow's sunrise wasn't an option. We couldn't risk being in the city that long.

Frost placed a hand on my lower back as I stood from my seat, gathering Stabitha, Slashley, and Slayla. I found it comical that he was trying to reassure me when he was stiffer than a corpse himself.

"I'm good," I told him, taking his hand from my back to give it a little squeeze. "Let's just get there."

If I was being honest, I needed to see Azrael.

We'd tried reaching him three times now to update him on our progress, and all three times there'd been no response. No return phone call. No text message.

Not even a fucking email.

He should have been there by now. The penthouse suite of the hotel.

"He's waiting for us, I'm sure of it," Frost said in a low whisper as Blake and Ethan shouldered their duffel bags and made their way to the front of the cabin.

I nodded, giving a little shrug that I hoped made it seem like I wasn't as worried as I felt inside. "I know."

Frost gave me a doubtful look before herding me forward.

Whispers echoed in the large space as we exited. The first of the vehicles had arrived, including the one we were to take.

Where the others looked very nondescript; mini-vans and hatchbacks and beat-up Hondas, ours was the SUV equivalent of a tank.

Larger than your usual SUV, it had blacked out bulletproof windows and a reinforced body that Azrael said could withstand a bomb, so it should be able to at least fend off vampire attack for a while.

I didn't think it was smart.

"Does anyone else think taking that monstrosity is asking for it?"

"Az insisted," Blake replied, and I couldn't help but notice that he seemed wary of using it also.

I shook my head. "No. We're taking that one."

I pointed to the silver Toyota. There would be hundreds of others just like it on the road. We'd blend right in.

"Rose," Ethan cautioned. "We don't deviate from the plan."

"Azrael said—" Frost began to jump to Ethan's defense, but I silenced him with a short glare.

I jumped down the last three steps of the stairs leading down from the plane and walked straight to the Toyota.

"*Rose*," Frost growled.

"Look," I snapped, dropping my weapons in the backseat. "If you can't see that taking that fucking thing is a bad idea on your own then I can't convince you. I know what Azrael said but *look at it*."

As one, my three guys glanced back at the other vehicle.

It was trying hard not to look suspicious, but as if the blacked-out windows weren't enough, the thing *looked* armored. The angular boxy shape of it. The fucking floodlights on top? *Jesus Christ.*

Azrael had managed to live thousands of years, sure, but he clearly didn't understand how to remain nondescript in the modern day. Probably he spent too much time in fucking caves instead of mingling with society.

Whereas Rafe owned the teeming streets of New York City. I didn't think a car like that would go unnoticed by him regardless of the impending war.

"Okay," Ethan pursed his lips. "I think she's right."

"Of course, I'm right."

"Um," a timid voice piped up from the loosely gathered vampires clinging to the edges of the hangar. "I'll take that one."

The vampire stood awkwardly, casting furtive glanced over us four as he approached with caution.

"It's a death wish," I told him.

"Maybe. But if it keeps eyes off you, milady, then it'll be well worth the risk."

My jaw tightened.

"You'll be tortured if you're caught."

It wouldn't accomplish much since Azrael compelled each and every one of them into silence in the case that that would happen. I didn't like it, but they all consented. None wanting to be the one to ruin everything we've worked towards. Even if Rafe himself tried to compel information out of them, it wouldn't be of any use. Az and Rafe were equally strong of mind and power of will. One could not undo another's compulsion. At least, not in such a short amount of time.

It would take days. Weeks even.

We only needed hours.

The vampire nodded. "It wouldn't be the first time. I can handle it."

Okay then.

"It's a good idea," Blake cut in. "But you go alone. We can't afford to risk a larger group."

I scanned the vampire's mind for thoughts of deceit or doubt but found only loyalty and a burning desire to be useful before finally letting death claim him. He knew there was a good chance he wouldn't live. He was hoping for it. *Hmm.*

"Alright then. You take the SUV. Don't forget to wipe the GPS as soon as you have the route memorized."

"Yes, milady."

"Azrael's going to be pissed," Ethan said under his breath as the lone vampire slid into the driver's seat of the armored vehicle.

"Azrael can suck it."

Frost barked a laugh and inclined his head to the Toyota. "Your chariot awaits *milady.*"

"Oh, piss off."

As EXPECTED, the newish silver Toyota made us all but invisible in the late-night NYC traffic. Didn't stop us all from being hella on edge though. The trip from the airstrip to the hotel wasn't long, even though the route mapped out for this vehicle was winding and took several turns that it didn't need to.

All in all, we managed to slide into the parking garage without ceremony, pulling into the lowest level near the pillar with a massive letter 'D' on it as instructed by the GPS.

"Do you think that guy made it?" I asked quietly as we gathered up our things and listened for foreign sounds, doing a visual sweep of the area.

At this hour of the night, there weren't any humans about. Nor any vampires nearby that I could feel. But the whole place had an eerie feel to it, nonetheless.

Walled in by cold concrete and slumbering vehicles. The shotty flickering blueish fluorescent lights weren't helping, either.

"Yeah," Ethan was the one to reply, giving me a tight smile. "I'm sure he did."

He didn't even sound like he believed himself and I saw how his fingers were clutched tight around the tablet he held at his side. The screen illuminated, though I couldn't see what he'd been looking at.

"Liar," I accused without any mirth and then slung Slashley over my shoulder. "Come on. Let's get inside before someone sees us."

"Azrael will have already cleared the building."

Unless he isn't inside it...

I didn't say it aloud because that would make it too real. Instead, I tucked some stray hair behind my ear and asked quietly, "Have you heard back from him at all?"

Ethan gave one short, sharp shake of his head.

Gasoline flooded my veins. Waiting to be lit.

"I have the hotel security cams," Ethan told the rest of us as we hustled into the door marked 'Exit' and made a sharp left to the bank of elevators. "Some of the others have already arrived and checked in."

That was a good sign.

Then why did I have this terrible fucking feeling in my chest?

The elevator doors clattered shut behind us, locking us in. My chest tightened. The parking garage had been alright, but elevators still made me itch, regardless of how much time I spent in that bunker.

The chipper music filtering in from the overhead speakers wasn't helping either.

Ethan punched the button for the lobby, instructing us to wait inside the elevator as he rushed across the marble tile foyer to the front desk.

A few vampires gave us conspiratorial nods as they made their way to the opposite elevator bank, bags, and room keys in hand.

Valentina gave a little wave as they entered from one elevator, clearing having just come up from the parking garage. I heaved a little sign of relief, not realizing how much I'd been worried about her. One of her mates lowered his hand for her, giving a little shake of his head. She flushed scarlet.

Sometimes I forgot how very young and naive she still was.

We needed all the help we could get tomorrow,

and I would not stop Valentina if she wanted to fight, but I made a mental note to give her the option to remain behind. Females were rare. And she'd already had one life taken from her too early. I didn't want to see her second chance ruined before it could even begin.

"Got it," Ethan said in a rush, sliding back into the elevator a moment later. He slid the keycard into the slot next to the button for the penthouse and the ring around it turned green.

When the door opened again some fifty floors later, it was to a wide, quiet space. The suite was the picture of luxury. The elevator opened into a living room the size of the gym back at the bunker. With a flatscreen bigger than a car, and lux white leather couches and chairs spread about.

Exotic flowers perched on side tables and the entire space was doused in a soft amber glow from the many expensive looking lamps and a few pod lights in the ceiling.

Taking up a good chunk of the space was a baby grand piano shined to a mirror polish, next to the wall-height windows looking out over the city.

I started at the sight, realizing with a sinking feeling in my gut that the building in the distance, about six blocks away, was Rafe's. I could just make out the shape of the roof where I'd jumped, and the side of its shining silver steel body.

"It's smart glass," Ethan explained before I could

rush forward in search of curtains. "We can see out, but no one can see inside."

I let loose the breath I'd been holding, but my rigid spine still did not relax.

"Where's Azrael?"

Not more than a second later he appeared, a tablet on his palm and a sneer on his lips.

"What part of *follow my instructions exactly* did you not understand?'

My relief at seeing him here, unharmed, waned almost instantly.

I bit back my first instinct to rush into his arms, because that was fucking ridiculous, and instead pasted a sneer on my own lips to match his.

"That fucking army tank you wanted us in would have gotten us killed."

His fiery eyes met mine. A muscle in his jaw ticked. "Can you not follow orders at all? Not even when it's for your own safety? For the safety of your mates?"

"Oh, fuck off," I scoffed, shedding off my jacket and tossing it to the wrought iron coat rack next to the door. "We got here didn't we."

"So stubborn. One day it's what'll get you killed."

Ethan cleared his throat, reminding me that they were all just two steps behind me, listening to us argue.

"Actually, Rose was right."

Ethan stepped forward, handing Azrael his tablet.

Lights flashed across his mismatched eyes as a

video was played for him, and I watched as they widened. As his face paled.

Unable to help myself, I stomped over to Azrael's side, jerking the tablet so I could see what Ethan was showing him, too.

Frost and Blake joined us, peering over my head.

I missed the start of the feed Ethan was replaying, but it was footage from a security camera. Not a traffic light cam, but maybe a camera out front of a building?

The vampires descended on the armored car. Our vamp decoy didn't try to make a getaway. He let the car roll to a stop. He *let* himself be taken. It took the vampires all of about twenty seconds to rip the driver's side door clean off the metal body and pull him out. For them to slide a black bag over his head and vanish into the night.

"Was that part of our route?" I breathed.

Ethan nodded. "He barely got more than six blocks into the nineteen-block route before they got him."

Azrael clicked the button to darken the screen and handed it back to Ethan, his adams apple bobbing in his throat.

Even though I was doing a little jig inside at being right, I didn't relish it as much as I thought it was. The look in Azrael's eyes was pure horror, even though he was clearly working hard to hide it.

Like it often did these days, whenever I wondered what one of my guys was thinking, my new power to read thoughts activated on its own.

She could have been taken...

I managed to catch the lone thought before Azrael felt my presence in his thoughts and threw me out. A hot bolt of pain shooting over my skull at the force of his ejection.

"Sorry," I muttered, catching his glare.

His face softened in the same second, though, and he let his gaze fall away from my face. "This will never happen again," he told me in a blank monotone. Something about the emotionless tone of his voice sent shivers racing over my back.

He sounded…

He sounded like his brother when he spoke like that.

I shrugged. "You fucked up. Whatever. I do it all the time."

He barked a forced laugh at that and wandered to the piano, sitting hard on the leather stool, and wiping his palms over the light scruff on his cheeks.

There was silence for a solid minute as the guys set to going over some of the hotel footage, checking to make sure everyone else made it inside the building.

"We need to get started," Azrael said, interrupting the guys' hushed conversation, tapping the screen of the other tablet still in his hands to check the time.

"We have less than four hours until sunrise. See that the recruits are all fed and armed. There's an arsenal of weapons in the hotel kitchen for those who prefer to fight with them and a full blood bag for each in the coolers.

"You'll have to wait until the last possible moment to begin inking in the elixir. We tip off the authorities to the fake bomb at exactly 6:45am. We march at dawn."

Ethan, Blake, and Frost share a look between themselves before each pair of eyes falls to me. I see, feel, and hear so many things in those eyes. In their minds.

They worry for me. For each other. And even, on some level, for Azrael and all of the vampires under our command. I share their sentiments, but we must all put them aside. None of us will be able to fight if we're all worrying about each other.

And now, on the precipice of it all, I understand their desire to lock me up away from danger. If I could live with betraying them like that, I'd fucking do it, too. I'd do anything to keep them safe.

My heart aches like a bleeding, broken thing in my chest, and I let it. Just for a second. Before I get myself back in line and lift my chin.

"You heard him," I say in the strongest voice I can muster. "Let's go."

"Not you," Azrael all but growls, his eyes casting me one furtive glance between falling back to the tablet in between his hands.

"Why the hell not?"

"This once, could you *not* argue with me, Rose?"

I clenched my teeth but didn't argue. We both might

be dead in a matter of a few hours, I supposed I could be reasonable for a minute.

"You need rest," Blake whispered in my ear, planting a soft kiss on my cheek before moving toward the door. "You didn't sleep at all last night. Get a couple of hours in while you can."

Ethan crushed me against him in a solid embrace, planting a swift kiss on the top of my head before he slipped his tablet into his bag and left with Blake.

Frost hovered, his jaw working as he regarded me and Azrael, and then me again.

"You take care of her," he finally said, directing the words at Azrael before he tugged me in to kiss me quick on the lips. "If she isn't fully satisfied by the time we return, I'll make you watch while I finish your job."

Blood rushed to my face when I realized what Frost was saying.

The bastard winked at me before closing the door behind himself, leaving me standing there like an idiot in the middle of the living room floor.

"Ro—"

"I need a shower," I blurted, rushing away from the living room. I had no idea where the fuck I was going, but I knew one of the doors near the kitchenette on the other side of the space would surely lead to a bathroom.

I needed to clear my head.

Thanks to three years of laser hair removal, my

pussy was smooth as silk, but if this was finally happening, I needed to shave my legs. I need to...

I didn't even know what I needed. A human minute, I supposed.

A dark chuckle sounded behind me as I disappeared through one of the doors, relieved to find it led to a bedroom with an adjoining bathroom.

I turned the water to near scalding and stood under the rain head for what could have been an eternity, just letting the water cascade down my body, loosening the tension in my muscles. Wash away my unease.

I wanted this. I wanted *him.* I had for a long ass time.

So then why the hell was I hesitating?

Through the gentle shushing sound of the water pouring over me, the first few notes of a song began to play. They made way for a slow building, haunting melody that took my breath away. Quietly, I shut off the water and stepped out of the shower, needing to hear it more clearly.

I could imagine Azrael's fingers stroking over the keys and I shuddered at the raw need to have those fingers touch me. To play *me* instead of the piano.

I eyed the stack of neatly rolled towels on the polished stone countertop and clenched my fists, leaving the bathroom without bothering to take one.

No more running. No more hiding.

No more pretending I didn't want him more than fucking oxygen.

It was agony these past few days, training and being near him, knowing I had the guys' blessing to make him mine. I needed to be sure it was what I wanted.

Something told me once we crossed that line there would be no going back.

But I was ready.

I'd been ready for a long time.

I left watery footprints on the hardwood floor as I exited the bathroom, walking silently across the kitchen area and through the arched ceiling into the living space once more.

Azrael's head was bent, bowing to the instrument as he played it, but his chin lifted as he sensed my approach, his fingers bringing the song tugging at my chest to a beautiful, yearning end.

"What was that?" I asked in a breath, my throat suddenly parched.

"My own composition," he replied as he stood, turning to face me. His lips parted as he took me in. The curve of my neck and swell of my breasts. The strong plane of my stomach and the way my thighs were pressed tightly together. "The first I've written in nearly one hundred years."

"I loved it."

His lips twitched into a grin and he gave an uncharacteristically shy nod. "I've named it *Requiem for a Rose*.

A mad blush clambered up my neck and I wet my lips, unable to look him in the eye as his admission played havoc in my chest.

The city lights made Azrael's mismatched eyes glow as he prowled closer. Anticipation tightened my chest. I was somewhat disappointed that Frost wasn't there with us after his confession to me about Az, but I was also grateful that he'd given us the chance to explore each other alone first. I'd imagined—for longer than I was willing to admit—what kind of lover Azrael would be and had gotten a glimpse when he fed from me.

But imagining wasn't enough.

I wanted to *know.*

He stopped inches from me, reaching up to tuck a damp strand behind my ear. His touch was gentle, but the fire it lit beneath my skin was not. It burned, consumed, fighting to break free.

Azrael's fingers trailed softly down my jaw and tipped my chin up. "I'm only going to ask this once—"

"Yes," I answered before he could get the question out.

My hands slid into his short hair, pulling him down to me. His lips met mine, feather-light at first, then firmer. More insistent. This wasn't a sudden impulse or a test of our desire for each other.

This was patience. Understanding.

A connection born of the darkness that dwelled in our hearts and had found a way to evolve together.

His stomach was hard under my fingertips, but the skin deliciously soft. I ran my hands up his chest and broke away long enough to shuck his shirt. Damn, he was a gorgeous man. When our lips came together again, my hunger deepened. Azrael pressed me close to him, one hand on my lower back and the other tangled in my hair, as his tongue explored my mouth.

There was a tenderness in his touch that I'd never thought him capable of once upon a time. Before I got to know him. Before I knew of the pain and loss he'd suffered in his long life.

I was the broken idiot who was falling for the broken ancient.

Azrael hands snaked low over my back until he cupped my ass, my legs wrapping around his waist instinctively as he lifted me off the floor. "Is there an off switch to your thoughts?"

"Just stay out of my head," I whispered, too turned on to care what he heard.

"Stop projecting," he growled against my lips.

He knelt on the bed and lowered me slowly, his hard length grinding against my wet pussy. I reached for his pants, but he caught my hand, bringing it to his face to press a kiss to the tip of each finger. With a captivated shudder, I laid back, awaiting his command, anxious to feel him. To know how our bodies would collide.

The corner of Azrael's mouth tilted up. He leaned over me, pressing kisses across my jaw, the spot below my ear, down my throat. Everywhere his lips touched, a new flame sprouted until I felt like I was going to combust. Only by sheer strength of will did I keep my little minx from taking over.

It took every ounce of self-control in my body not to attack him like a lioness would her prey.

I gasped when his tongue flicked out, tasting my skin. My fingers found his soft hair again and I felt him grin against my collarbone as he continued down. His lips skimmed across the tops of my breasts, leaving goosebumps in their wake. My nipples were stiff peaks, displaying for him their desire for attention.

But he went around, kissing the underside of each breast. If I didn't know any better, I'd think he intended to torture me. Kissing every part of me except the parts that needed his attention the most. I fought the urge to squirm, to yank his head to said parts and demand it.

A deep chuckle vibrated in his chest and rippled across my nerve endings. The fucker was still in my head.

"You're still projecting."

Before I could muster a response, his mouth closed around my right nipple. Static danced across my skin, a ballet of exquisite pleasure. My back arched into him and a quiet whimper escaped my throat. I wasn't sure if this slow, gentle pace was his usual style, but it certainly wasn't what I was used to.

Though I wasn't complaining. Too much.

Teeth scraped across my nipple, followed by the wet heat of his tongue. I squeezed my eyes shut, breaths coming in short puffs as I tried to stay in control of myself. It was a most elegant torment. Heat uncoiled from my stomach and slithered through my core to my throbbing clit.

I hadn't realized my hand had moved that way until Azrael caught it. He released my nipple with one last flick of his tongue, then put my hand on my own boob. Through the haze of lust, I caught his smirk as he kissed his way across to the other one. His hand stayed over mine, squeezing and massaging, as he took my left nipple into his mouth.

My thighs squeezed together around him and I shifted, trying to create some kind of friction down there, but he pressed his weight down to keep me from moving. Dammit, I was going to go insane before he made it that far. His tongue swirled delicately, and I felt the brush of a fang that sent a jolt of lightning through my body.

I released a shuddering breath, gripping the bedspread in my left fist while he continued to hold my right hand hostage. Every cell, every fucking molecule was lit up like a Christmas tree. I grit my teeth against another whimper as he let go, then brushed his nose down into the valley between my breasts. His tongue darted out, sampling the flesh there.

"Please, Az," I pleaded, my voice barely above a whisper. Taste me. Bite me.

Fuck me.

He hummed, and I could hear the amusement in that simple sound. My hips bucked as his weight shifted, moving to press kisses across my stomach. He was so close I could practically feel his breath washing over my pussy. I tried to keep my thoughts locked down, but my head was foggy with desire.

An image flashed through my mind, a memory of me laying on him as he fed on me. My ass grinding against his crotch. His hand cupping my boob. I'd wanted so badly to ignore my argument with Frost and take him that day.

Azrael growled and the vibration so close to my clit made it throb harder. I glanced down and saw him watching me, gaze half-lidded. He gripped my thighs and I braced myself to orgasm as soon as he touched me, but then I felt his lips on my knee. My eyes snapped back open to see a faint smile on his face as he kissed his way up my leg.

It was my turn to growl. I loved the attention, but there was a limit to my patience.

He nipped at the delicate flesh of my inner thigh. I bit my lip and, before he could pluck the thought from my head, I started massaging both breasts and moaned. If he was going to play games, maybe I could force his hand. He paused to watch for a second, and a wicked grin stretched across his beautiful face.

I cried out in earnest as his mouth finally latched onto my sex. Firecrackers exploded behind my eyelids. All the build-up, the tension coiling in every nerve, crashed down like a tsunami. It hit so hard, so unexpectedly, that my eyes watered with the force of it. Every flick, every hard stroke of his tongue kept me rolling beneath the surface. My breath was trapped in my chest, and I felt his hand slide up my stomach and press down, holding me still.

Then my lungs released just long enough for me to get another breath before he sucked my clit into his mouth. Black spots danced at the edges of my vision as I was pulled back under another wave of ecstasy.

What the ever-loving fuck was he doing to me?

I opened my mouth, but my words were stuck in my throat. Azrael hummed again and my whole body jerked in his grasp. I fought to get my thoughts in line.

Fuck. Me. Now.

His tongue never let up, but beneath the pounding in my chest, I heard the rustle of cloth. His pants. *Yes. Please!*

Cool air swept over my wet pussy. Azrael wiped his mouth and crawled back up my body, his enormous erection hanging heavily between us. Everywhere his skin met mine sent aftershocks of pleasure through me. It was almost like he was the orgasm. Maybe those were the kinds of tricks you learned over a thousand years. How to play the human body like a piano, making it tremor with every note you hit.

"And did I hit your notes well?" he asked, brushing his nose against mine.

I groaned and stole his lips, the taste of me on his tongue so fucking erotic. His dick pressed against my sensitive bud and I shifted for him. He didn't ask, as he said he wouldn't, but he did meet my eyes. There was a question in them that I answered with the press of my legs against his ass.

Azrael eased into me slowly, giving me time to adjust. He was in no rush, like he had all the time in the world. I, however, was growing impatient. I rolled my hips in time with him until he was seated and the fullness in me nearly took my breath away. A strangled gasp escaped my throat as he continued his slow thrusts, each one hitting deep inside.

My nails dug into the skin around his shoulder blades, but he didn't react. It seemed impossible that such unhurried, leisurely movements could stoke a fire back up, but the tightening in my core said otherwise. I liked it fast, rough, wild.

This was something else entirely. Controlled. Tempered.

But I wanted to shatter.

He grunted quietly and picked up his pace, leaning on his left arm to grab my thigh with his right. A flicker of thought came to me, but it wasn't mine. Azrael was intentionally holding back. For me.

I understood then. Vampires were incredibly strong the older they got. He was being careful because he didn't want to shatter me in the literal sense. Control was more than necessary with a human; it was required.

"I'll heal," I said, taking his face into my hands. "Don't hold back for me. I want you and everything that comes with that."

He huffed a laugh and pressed his forehead to mine. "Stay out of my head."

Words eluded us after that. The demon he had leashed behind that calm exterior broke free and slammed into me so wildly that I thought my womb would bruise.

I didn't care. I was lost to the quickening sensation, the untamed euphoria each stroke promised. He was bliss in physical form, and I wanted it all. I circled my hips, grinding on his shaft, increasing the friction. His arm wrapped around my waist, pulling me harder against him, changing the angle of his thrusts only slightly, but enough to feel the difference.

The noise that ripped from my throat was an unrestrained combination of a primal growl and a rapturous cry. "Shattered" came far short of describing what he did to me. My body was fire and lightning and agony and exhilaration. Each aftershock was an orgasm unto itself. I wasn't sure how much more I could handle without melting into a boneless puddle.

Suddenly, the world spun, and I was sitting on his lap. He gripped my ass, driving me down on his dick before I automatically took over. I was dizzy with desire, but he held me close, tilting my head to the side. He was going to bite me.

Fuck yes.

His lips blazed down the column of my throat and I felt the press of his teeth on my shoulder. My fingers tangled in his hair, encouraging him, begging him. The black spots dancing at the edge of my vision came back in full force, my breaths rough and uneven as I rode him toward another blissful end. The moment his teeth broke the skin, his grip tightened, and his length twitched and hardened further inside me.

The room went fuzzy, and my head felt like it was floating above my shoulders. Azrael grunted, his thrusts becoming erratic, and lava coated my insides, filled my veins, warmed my chest. He ripped me apart with every orgasm, only to piece me back together and rip me apart again. I was hanging onto consciousness by a thread.

His teeth slid free and he licked the wound as it started to heal. I leaned heavily against him, nuzzling his face, and he laid us back in the bed.

My every key had been played masterfully.

15

Sleep would've been impossible, no matter how much I wished I could've curled up next to Az on the insanely comfortable bed. We both knew it.

So, instead of trying at all, we laid there for a time. Content in each other's company. Trading thoughts every so often until the minutes turned to hours and the energy in the room began to shift. The atmosphere thick with what was to come.

The battle rushed toward us like a spray of bullets. There was no longer any avoiding it.

At some point, we both quietly rose from the tangle of our naked bodies and began to dress.

"What are our chances?" I asked as I did up my boots, unable to look him in the eyes.

He paused before replying. "If it's true that he has us

outnumbered two to one...about fifty-fifty. We have the advantage of the sun."

"But he has bullet-proof glass..."

"Bullet-proof. Not vampire proof."

I chuckled darkly.

"It would be easier if we could simply," Azrael paused, gaze flitting to me and then away again. "Blow it up," he finished, one brow raised.

He was right, of course. It *would* be easier. And with the streets in a ten-block radius cleared, there would be little in the way of human casualties.

Except...the girls. Raphael's compelled *wives*, living like sex slaves in the top of his tower. I owed it to them to try and save them.

That was where I was headed. Once we got the go ahead, the guys and I would prioritize saving them first while Azrael went with the rest of our recruits in search of Raphael, ending the lives of any who stood in their path.

Once the women were safely out of the building, I couldn't give two shits what they did. I knew Ethan had some explosives ready. I didn't know how many, or if they would be enough to raise the building to the ground. Or if blowing Raphael up would even kill him, but it was worth a shot.

Az assured us that cutting the head off the snake and burning its remains would see the job done. So, as long as the blast tore him apart, it should do the trick.

"I can't abandon them," I said in a low, even tone. "I won't."

I didn't have to explain what I meant. Guaranteed the fucker was still in my head, like always. He knew exactly who I was talking about.

"I know." Azrael appeared at my side, his hand raising to gently cup my cheek. "It's taken me some time to understand. You're such a contradiction. You wouldn't hesitate to cut down anyone who crossed you. Anyone who deserved it. But you would risk your own life to save these women."

"Because they don't deserve what happened to them. They deserve freedom. *Life.*"

Azrael's eyes shone, even though on some level, I could tell he still didn't fully comprehend my mercy. The darkness that'd been eating at him for the last thousand years wouldn't allow it. But he was clearly trying and that was enough for me.

He lowered his head until our crowns met, his thumb brushing over my cheekbone. "So do you."

Something clenched in my belly and I grit my teeth against the rise of emotion in my throat.

"And I'll have it. As soon as he's dead."

I drew back from Az, fixing him with a hard stare. "This time, you can't hesitate."

His jaw tensed.

"If you have the opportunity, you *must* end him."

I'd do it myself if I could. I'd die trying. But I needed to know that he wouldn't back down this time. He let his brother get away once. We couldn't let that happen again.

His heated stare bored into me as his upper lip curled.

"Raphael is dead to me already," Azrael told me through gritted teeth. "He was dead the moment he lifted a finger against you."

I nodded once, sharply, before turning my attention to the bedside alarm clock.

"We need to get ready."

One hour stood between us and sunrise.

One hour left to live.

One hour to freedom.

Only fate could decide.

16

"*T*he fuck are you doing?"

Frost's gravelly voice almost had me slicing my face open.

"You almost made me cut my eyeball out," I hissed back before returning to the task at hand. I replaced the edge of the short blade against the corner of my eye, using it as a guide to draw the perfect winged liner onto my eyes.

"Makeup?" Blake chided, strolling into the bathroom behind Frost. I could sense Ethan hovering the room outside. "Are you actually doing your makeup right now? We're heading out in twenty."

I groaned, lowering the knife. "I need to focus. Could you shut up for two seconds?"

They quieted and I was able to draw a wing on the other eye. They turned out equal on the first try without any adjustments and I took that to be a good omen, smiling at my reflection.

I hadn't only done the liner. I'd also coated my lashes in mascara and concealed the bags under my eyes. A call down to hotel reception with a promise of a very large tip also got me a killer shade of blood red lip stain to complete the look.

My audience stared with varying degrees of confusion as I turned to them, not seeking approval, but happy to get it nonetheless when their eyes roamed over my leather-clad body and polished black hair tied back in a braided bun.

"I fight better when I look good," I explained with a shrug.

The explanation was met with more confusion. Raised brows and puckered lips.

"It's a chick thing," I huffed. "You wouldn't get it."

Had they said twenty minutes? How long had I been in here?

I cleared my throat, trying to quell the uneasiness in my stomach. When it wouldn't go away on its own, I allowed it to propel me forward.

Throwing myself at them, my guys wrapped themselves around me like a cocoon. I buried my face in the clean linen scent of Blake while Frost held me from behind and Ethan joined in, huddling against us all. He planted a kiss on my forehead and sighed.

We stayed like that for a few minutes. Just...holding each other.

Any other time, I might have complained at how tightly they held me. I may have told them I could barely breathe. But I didn't feel claustrophobic with their arms around me. I felt safe. And loved.

Not so long ago those feelings were entirely foreign to me, and no matter what happened today, I'd have those feelings to hold onto. Because of my guys, I'd known love.

This right here, the entanglement of our bodies, was more intimate than fucking could ever be.

"It's time."

The two words sliced through the false sense of calm and I peered grudgingly upward from Blake's chest and part of Frost's bicep to see Azrael standing several feet away. His arms clasped behind his back. A solemn look drawing down the corners of his mouth. His eyes dark.

"Everything is in place. SWAT has sealed the immediate area and I've compelled them to stay back."

"I've disabled all cameras within a nine-block radius of the building," Ethan confirmed, pulling back from us.

"We've used up every ounce of ink we had," Blake added. "The tattoos are filled and large. They should hold."

Azrael nodded. "Then we're ready."

We came apart slowly, like petals unfurling from the heart of a Rose.

Time to show these fuckers just how dangerous a single flower could be.

IT PROVED a simple task to get past the SWAT blockades and into the evacuated zone. I didn't even have to speak to compel the officers to make way for us and then immediately forget we were ever there.

My fist clenched and I sent a silent thank you to Amala as the building came into view ahead of us. Her spell seemed to still be in full force and effect. And it combined with the insane levels of adrenaline coursing through my veins made me feel abso-fucking-lutely invincible.

Even Azrael couldn't seem to stop shooting me prideful glances as we moved past the blockades. Like he was the one walking among a superior being, instead of the other way around.

I felt unstoppable. And it was a good thing because nothing less would keep me alive.

My blood hummed as we approached the tall column of steel and glass. It jutted up from the blacktop like a knife, glinting with almost blinding light as the sun cast strong amber rays over the mirror-surface.

We didn't know exactly how long we had. The tattoos inked into our army's flesh could last thirty more minutes or only ten. The pale faces of my men standing shoulder to shoulder next to me were set as though carved in stone.

Their thoughts pulsed with a single-minded, malicious purpose.

Kill them all.

Protect Rose.

No matter the cost...

And ahead, as I sent out my mental feelers, I found that I could hear the voices of those within the building, too.

Azrael and I shared a look.

They knew we were here.

"Ready?"

I knotted my fingers through his, giving a short squeeze before letting go and drawing my stakes. "Ready."

I turned my head, casting my murderous gaze over the vampires at our backs. There was no need for words. I could hear it in their minds. They were ready. They were fucking chomping at the bit.

This was what happened when you kept monsters caged for too long.

"Now!" I shouted and braced my body as Frost grabbed me by the arm and thigh and flung me at the building, hurtling me way too many stories in the air. I twisted midair, positioning my stakes and the heels of my boots for impact.

The glass window shattered at the impact and I

rolled into a crouch on the linoleum tile inside, knowing my guys were right behind me.

The ear-splitting sounds of the battle raging on the ground level echoed all around me and I fixated my mind on my task. One thing at a time. I couldn't accomplish anything if I was worrying about Azrael and the others.

We all anticipated that Rafe would hole up with his strongest bodyguards at his sides. He would wait until his newly refreshed army took out the vast majority of ours before he'd join the fight. Like the coward he is.

"Which way," Frost bellowed, eyes searching the corridor for signs of attack. Where Blake preferred to carry a steel bat, and Ethan had a vest of short daggers crossed over his chest, Frost liked to use nothing but his bare hands in a fight.

I could see them clenching, aching to tear something apart.

"That way," I gestured, spurring into action. We had the advantage of surprise up here. None expected us to split up.

Rafe wouldn't have anticipated that I'd care enough to go after the women first.

But the element of surprise was lost now. Any who could be spared would be sent up after us. Especially once Rafe knew I was among them.

We rushed through to the right and I paused, second guessing myself. I'd only been in these hallways once before.

"Rose," Blake warned, and I gritted my teeth.

Shit.

I saw the exit sign ahead and a burst of clarity came to my mind. "It's that way."

Only problem was, there were no windows that way. And there were no windows in the room where Rafe kept his wives, either.

When the door finally came into view, a pit yawned open in my gut, remembering the excruciating agony of my escape. Remembering Rafe's threats to kill them all if I didn't cooperate with his demands.

Please. Please still be alive.

Frost had the door down, hanging by a hinge in two seconds flat. I could've told him there was no need for Rafe to lock it, but oh well.

Screams filled the air as we entered, a waft of essential oils and soapy bathwater choking off my airways. I didn't think I'd ever heard a more beautiful sound.

Hastily, I rushed to the first of them I could find, grabbing Penny by the arms. "It's me," I shouted, drawing up all of my energy and letting it flood my compulsion, praying it would be strong enough for its purpose. "Come with us. We're taking you away from here."

There was a second where I thought she would argue, her lips parting and eyes widening in fear, Rafe's compulsion clinging to her mind, but then the telltale glaze of my compulsion washed over her beautiful blue eyes and she nodded.

One down…

Seven to go.

My chest tightened.

Where were the others?

"Where's Luz?"

Distantly, she replied. "Luz? Who's that?"

My heart ached as I passed her off to Ethan, trying not to believe that we were too late to save her. She could still be alive. She could still be here somewhere, I just had to find her. Just because Rafe had clearly compelled the girls to forget her didn't mean I had.

"Get her out."

One by one, we went through them. Me compelling them and the guys taking turns hurtling them down to the street outside via our busted window. If they stayed in the sun outside, they should be safe until this was all over.

Then I could personally see to it that they returned to some semblance of normal life.

They looked more frail than the last time I'd seen them. Gaunt and hollow.

I wondered if Rafe had stopped feeding them and it only poured more gasoline on the flames of my rage.

"Rose?" Grace said as she came out of the bathroom, recognizing me before I could reach her.

She was the last one.

The others were all already out and I was in shock that no one had tried to stop us yet. Rafe had to know I was here by now. He'd be able to see into the minds of the others that I was among the group leading the charge. That it was my blood that made them impervious to sunlight. He had to want me more than he ever did before.

Right?

Cold dread filled my veins as I rubbed warmth into Grace's arms and compelled her to go with Frost. I tugged her into a quick hug before letting her go. If nothing else, at least I could say that I'd followed through on my promise. I'd saved them.

If this was some sort of trap and we were about to go down in a blaze of fucking glory, then at least I had that one victory.

A ball formed in my throat as Ethan and Blake reappeared, crossing paths with Frost as he football carried Grace from the room in a sprint.

"They're coming," Blake hissed, fingers denting the metal on the handle of his bat.

He was right, I realized.

The sound of their approach was all but silent, but I could hear their thoughts. I counted the different minds in my head, flipping my stakes in my palms back to kill mode.

"There are eleven of them," I told the guys just as Frost returned.

"They all outside?"

"In the sun on the sidewalk. They're safe," Frost confirmed.

I grinned, feeling more ready now than I had in

days. "Then let's go slay some monsters."

Frost's returning grin was all teeth.

"Lead the way, Rosie."

"With motherfucking pleasure."

I raced from the room, following the echo of foreign voices like a glowing string in the dark.

"Stairwell," I announced as we rounded a bend, searching the immediate area for a window to smash. "There."

Frost kicked it out just as the vamps crashed through the door. I staked one before the sunlight could even hit them, and then it was all hisses and screeching. The smell of burning immortal flesh ripe in the air as they retreated back down, away from the light.

But that wouldn't do.

I couldn't have them cowering when I killed them. I needed them vicious. I needed a challenge.

This...well, this was pathetic.

"*Rose*," Ethan called out as I stepped out of the light and into the stairwell, daring them with my eyes to move forward.

Raw power rippled beneath my skin and I felt electrified from the inside out.

As they rushed forward, I let that power flood my body.

"*Stop.*" The single word ripped from my lips in a feral roar and I had the satisfaction of watching every muscle in their bodies freeze. They stopped *everything*.

They stopped moving. Stopped hissing and shouting. Stopped *breathing*.

I turned to the guys for approval and frowned, losing my focus. I hadn't just frozen the vampires in the stairwell. I'd frozen them, too.

The rush of power waned, and sharp pain exploded into my shoulder as my compulsion came undone. My body crashed to the ground, my head snapping hard against the metal edge of a stair as I went down. A boot connected with my stomach and I heard someone shout about needing to take me alive.

Not a fucking chance.

Even though I felt like I was about to hurl from the boot to the gut and I was pretty damned sure the vamp had broken at least one rib, I curled my body in before kicking my legs out. The swift kick took down two vampires, snatching their legs out from under them.

I'd dropped one stake somewhere in the fall. But I still had Stabitha and one was more than enough.

My guys attacked with precision and grace. Slaughtering the vampires in the path to get to me like they were plucking daisies.

I sank my stake into the one trying to drag me down the steps, using his own momentum against him to send us flying into the wall at the bottom of the stairs. My stake went through him and partially into the drywall, splattering blood over the side of my face and neck as he gurgled to his end.

Spinning in anticipation of another attack, I stilled

before swinging, finding only my guys standing amid a floor of carnage. Bathed in the blood of the vampires now bowing lifelessly at their feet.

And there must be something seriously fucking wrong with me because I didn't think I'd ever been more turned on. Even while they were staring at me with anger flashing in their eyes.

"Sorry," I winced. "I didn't mean to—"

Frost cut me off with a growl.

"Maybe let's *not* test out the limits of your abilities today, love?" Blake said, stepping over a corpse to get to me. He pressed two fingers against my temple, examining the wound there. It leaked a steady stream of blood, but I could already feel it healing.

"Are you good to keep going?" Ethan asked plainly and Blake cut him a glare. I knew if he had his way, he'd take me out of the fight right here and now.

I made a flippant sound and bent to retrieve my fallen stake, covering up a pained grunt with a laugh when the movement made my freshly broken rib ache. "Good? I'm *great*. Let's go get this over with."

Ethan looked doubtful at me but didn't argue.

"There are more coming from below," I told them, hearing the faint whisper of several new minds, one of them counting steps as they ascended.

"Let's get down to the ground level," Frost growled, throwing a fist through the wall. He had a man-sized hole ripped into it in less than five seconds. I squinted into the daylight, holding up a hand to shield my eyes. I didn't want to admit it, but my vision was hazed. The hit I'd taken to the head on the stairs had been harder than I let on. And the bruising grip the vampire used to haul me down by my shoulder had obviously done a number on the joint.

"If we can evacuate ours from the building, we can end this here and now," Ethan said, making us pause. "There's a duffel of C4 on the roof of the building next door. I planted it last night."

Frost and Blake shared a look.

"That was fucking risky," I said, incredulous and a little pissed off that he'd risked his life and our whole operation while I was busy fucking Azrael.

Ethan's lips pressed together, but he did not apologize. "If we can get it and get our people out, then we can blow this building to kingdom come. It can be *over*."

Something told me it wouldn't be so easy, but I nodded. It was the easiest option, even if it killed me a little that I may not be able to get my hands any more bloody than they already were.

A waste of good eyeliner if you asked me.

"You get the explosives," I pointed at Ethan. "We'll start evacuating."

"Meet us out front," Frost nodded to Ethan, scooping me up into his chest before he stepped out the hole he created and sent us falling to the ground. My stomach heaved at the long drop and all the breath rushed from my lungs.

ELENA LAWSON

Frost tipped me back onto my feet as he rose from the crouch, revealing a web of new cracks in the sidewalk. I spied the women from upstairs huddled on the street corner down the way and grimaced. I wished I'd had the presence of mind to push a few blankets into their arms as I sent them out, but it was still plain to see for anyone looking that they were naked.

And dazed as they were with compulsion, they didn't seem to care.

First order of business once this was over—get them some goddamned clothes.

Blake and Frost flanked me on either side as we moved to enter the building from the front. It became increasingly clear that the best way to cover this up was to blow the whole thing to ash. There was too much carnage.

A carpet of lightly smoking vampire bodies littered the front entry and deeper into the bowels of the building I could hear the fight continue to rage on. They'd retreated down as we thought they would.

Down into the basement where the sun couldn't reach unless we ripped down all the floors above.

But by the look of the dead up here, Azrael and the rest of our troop had already managed to decimate at least half of their force. I saw only a handful of faces I recognized among the lifeless bodies as we hurried around and through them, making our way to the elevator shaft at the edge of the space. That was a good sign.

For the first time in a long time, I let myself hope that this could truly be *it*. The end of Raphael's tyrannical reign. The end of an era of rogue vampires. The beginning of a new era of order and peace.

We were going to win.

"Don't look so smug," Frost warned with a snarl in his upper lip. "The fight isn't over yet."

I checked myself, knowing he was right. This was no time to get cocky.

I felt more than heard Ethan as he entered the building behind us, a fat duffel slung over his shoulder.

"Plant it," I ordered. "We'll be back up in a minute."

Blake jumped down the shaft first, without even checking to see if the elevator itself was above or below. I checked. It had clearly been dismantled and lay crooked and broken three floors below, where the deafening roar of vampire war drifted up from below.

Once I was sure I wasn't about to be flattened by an elevator car, I jumped down after him, followed by Frost as Ethan rushed to set up the explosives in the most optimal places to bring the building down.

Watch your back, I sent the silent command back up to him, hating that we were leaving him without someone to watch it for him. I'd scanned the entire main floor for signs of immortal life and found none. He should be fine, I told myself as my feet connected with the roof of the mangled elevator car and I gaped, staring into the pits of hell.

17

*I*t was near impossible to distinguish friend from foe and I was glad of my new ability to read minds or I might have wound up killing just as many of our own troops as I did the enemy's.

The fight had taken out most of the load bearing walls and it was a structural wonder that the building hadn't already fallen. The space clearly once used for maintenance and storage was now a dust-filled chasm belowground.

The heat of exerted bodies swirled in the air, along with the stench of death. As blood curdling screams, guttural snarls, and the sounds of war echoed deafeningly through the space.

I tried to find Azrael in the fray, but I couldn't see him.

An anvil dropped in my stomach and I pressed my

teeth hard together, feeling for him instead. Frost
fought off two attackers while Blake stayed tucked in
close to my side, protecting me while I used my mind
to search for him.

My eyes flew open a second later and my head
snapped to the right. He was under attack.

Unthinking, I lunged from the elevator car, flipping
my body into a roll, and kicking out an ankle as I
landed. The vampire went down, and I had him staked
before he even knew what hit him.

My guys and I carved a path of carnage on our way
to Azrael, and I stiffened, feeling the definite creep of
my sixth sense as it clawed up my spine. It was Rafe.

I was sure of it.

He was coming.

"Rose, watch out!"

The warning saved me just in time and I hit the
floor, ducking what might have been a fatal blow. I
swung the vampire's legs out from under him, but he
was faster and stronger than the others I'd taken out to
this point.

He tried to meet my eyes as he lunged. His lips parting. He was going to try to compel me.

Not so long ago, I'd have been terrified at the
thought. I'd have blamed myself for letting myself stare
into his eyes. For letting myself be compelled before I
could do the compelling. Now, I smiled.

I tsked the vampire as he froze in place, held for a

split second by my compulsion, but it was all I needed. I had my katana out in a flash, and his head lobbed to the floor with a sickening squelch.

"Az!" I called, able to see him through the throng now.

Heads turned.

For some, it was the distraction our side needed to finish off their foes.

But for others…

Bloodthirsty stares turned on me and I realized my mistake.

The ones nearest to me had already surmised who I was and attacked. They could hear the beating of my heart. Smell my blood.

Shouting just told the rest of them that I was here, too.

They descended in a wave of fangs and claws, burying us in a matter of seconds.

My vision darkened, taking me to the black place where my body knew only survival. Running on pure adrenaline and reflex, I managed to cut a path through.

A grunt behind me told me Blake had taken a bad blow and I used the opening to drag him out, calling to Frost to *fucking move*.

We didn't have much time before their tattoos would stop working. We needed to get outside. We needed to torch this shit.

I didn't think the blast from the explosives Ethan

had planted upstairs would reach three levels down, but the vampires who remained down here would be buried in rubble. And if they tried to claw their way out, they'd be lit up by the sun.

It would have to do.

Even if I had to dig through the rubble to find Rafe and make sure he was dead myself when the others had to seek shelter, I would.

I'd personally see to his fucking barbeque.

"Azrael!" I called again, knowing no matter how many he was fighting off, he would hear me. "Fall back!"

In my head, I shouted. *Let's blow this popsicle stand.*

It was at that moment, I found him, a marvel of muscle and savagery.

His clothes had been torn from his perfectly unmarked body. His every muscle coiled as he cut down anyone who drew even remotely near. Tearing and hacking and tossing like the vampires rushing him were toys and he was their terrible puppeteer.

Damn.

He met my stare for an instant and in it was conveyed his agreement.

He was coming.

Now how to get the rest of them to follow?

I couldn't see Valentina or the vampire who professed his loyalty to me before we left the bunker. I'd have trusted either of them to help round up the others.

Compelling, wouldn't work, I wouldn't be able to separate friend from foe...

Oh my god.

I didn't have to.

A deviant smile slithered over my lips, and it must have been terrifying for the way Frost looked at me.

Sending out my mental feelers in *all* directions, I blasted the command like a shockwave to every mind in the room. Picturing it like a signal from a cell tower sending a mass text message.

Ping motherfuckers.

Incoming message: Time to go outside and play.

As one, the vampires stilled, and I wanted to kiss Azrael for forcing me into mental aerobics day and night since our encounter with Amala. Between her gift of heightened power and his instruction, I'd become something *other*.

Something *more* than Azrael or Rafe could ever be.

Acknowledging it only seemed to strengthen it.

The only one unencumbered by my compulsion was Azrael. He halted in his fight, chest heaving and eyes wild. His blue eye vivid against his red-stained skin.

There was enough blood covering his body that if I didn't know any better, I'd have to assume he bathed in it.

"Rose..." he trailed off, my name a reverent whisper on his lips as he fought my compulsion hard enough to break it.

Several others struggled, but it was no use. They couldn't deny me.

As though retracting a few claws, I withdrew my compulsion, careful to only withdraw it from the minds of Ethan and Frost.

As one, they gasped, twitching as they stared between Azrael and I, and then to the other vampires, who were all dutifully making their way to the either end of the body and rubble strewn lower level, where twin exit signs glowed above doors leading up.

"How are you doing this?" Blake asked in a breath, his face paler than polished ivory.

It wasn't without effort, that was for sure. Holding them all to my will felt a little bit like tearing my brain in two, but I was managing alright.

"Let's just get outside," I muttered through clenched teeth, trying to hide the amount of pain this was causing me.

Azrael knew though, and he drew me into his blood-soaked side, helping me toward the stairs. I didn't have the energy to block him and keep focus on my compulsion.

"I've got you," he said, leading me up and out. Using his own compulsion to force the vampires clogging the arteries of the stairwell to either side so that the four of us could pass through.

He had us outside only a moment later, lifting me easily from the floor to rush me out. He didn't let me go until we were firmly in the sunlight, just fifteen paces in front of the building where the vampires had already begun streaming out.

The ones not bearing the black rose tattoo cried. They struggled against my power. And as each of them met the sun, they burned.

An unexpected pang of guilt hollowed my stomach and Azrael held fast to me, whispering against my ear. "Only a very small few were compelled to be here against their will," he said. "Nearly all of them share the beliefs of my brother. This earth is better off without them."

I dipped my head, shoving back the feelings trying to break through the hard casing around my heart.

There were always casualties in war. Some who deserved it, and others who didn't. I didn't have the strength to pick through the minds of each as they joined their ashen brethren outside to decipher which were worth saving.

I took solace in placing the blame squarely on Rafe's shoulders for their deaths. If he hadn't compelled them to follow him, then I wouldn't have to kill them. At the very least, we'd have to equally share the blame.

Though I doubted a monster like him even knew what the word meant.

"Where's…" I spluttered, feeling a dribble of blood leak down from my nose a roll over my lips. Similar drops leaked from my ears and I struggled to hold on just a little longer, focusing on the single task of forcing every vampire that'd been in that room with us outside. There were only a few left now. Just another minute.

Azrael raised a brow at me, and I had to dig through my compacted thoughts to remember what I'd even been about to say. "Where's..." I choked. "Raphael?"

His jaw tightened, but he didn't reply.

Shit. That wasn't good.

"What the hell is happening to her? What's going on?" Ethan's panicked voice took over my senses as he ripped me from Azrael's side, checking me over for injuring. The jarring movement interrupted my focus for a second and I lost it.

The tenuous hold I had on their minds slipped like sand through my fingers and I crumpled, seeing double.

"*Idiot,*" I heard Azrael hiss at him. "She only needed another second."

"She was *dying.*"

"Hardly. She was *transcending.*"

I smirked through the discomfort, forcing my wobbly legs to stand. "Eth, I'm alright. I just need a second."

I glanced up, peering through the soot and smoke clogged air to see that there was still a decent sized group of vampires inside. The rest of our troop had fled the rest of the way outside when my compulsion broke, but the others stayed back, hidden away from direct sunlight in the shadows.

There were still at least fifty of them, and Rafe was still somewhere in the building, too.

"Light them up," I croaked, staring into Ethan's glinting honey eyes, and seeing fire.

He passed me off to Frost, who I batted away as I regained my vision and footing. I was *fine*.

Or at least, I hoped I would be. My body felt weak and useless. Like I was a lump of skin and bones with no muscle to hold me up.

Heal, I commanded myself. *And hurry the fuck up about it.*

This fight wasn't over yet. Not until they all burned.

Ethan's fingers clasped over his cellphone and he thumbed the screen, bringing up the dial pad.

Frost gripped me by the arm, hauling me backward, out of the blast radius, I assumed.

I found the girls still huddled on the sidewalk half a block down and used what remained of my energy to send a compelling command to them. They needed to get back, too. I compelled them to go two blocks south-east. There, they'd be taken into police custody. I'd worry about getting them free and back on their feet later. At least they'd be safe.

"You missed one."

His voice was like ice in my veins. Flash-freezing the lingering flames in my core. And I didn't know how I'd ever not been able to see the glaring differences between them, because as my eyes fell to land on Raphael, standing just out of range of the sunlight in the crumbled entryway of his grand building, I saw nothing of his twin.

They didn't sound alike.

They didn't look alike.

They were nothing alike at all.

The monster with his fist knotted in Luz's hair as her naked body writhed for escape was no more like my Azrael than a serpent was like a lion.

I saw *red*.

Ethan's finger hovered over the call button and for one heart stopping moment I heard his thoughts. His intent to push it anyway. And I lunged for him, knocking the phone from his grip.

It clattered to the pavement and I glared at him.

"Luz is in there, Ethan."

"Let her go," I hollered across the gorge of death between us as what remained of our army took up their places at our backs. They were spent and blood-ied, but all of them ready for another fight.

Raphael laughed at my demand and I shivered, feeling the undeniable tremor of powerful vampires creep over me. They surrounded Raphael, coming up to stand to either flank.

Fifty.

No. Closer to eighty.

The strongest of them.

The oldest.

We'd been right about Raphael keeping his most powerful at his sides while the rest of his followers sacrificed themselves in his name. And it made sense. Why killing them all had been so easy. Why none save for Azrael were able to even moderately withstand my compulsion. Because they were his weakest links.

We couldn't fight them.

We were barely eighty ourselves now by the look of things, and as unfortunate as it was to admit to myself in the dark recesses of my mind; ours were not of the same caliber as his.

They were not handpicked from a mass of hundreds for their strength and age. We didn't discriminate as we built our force. We'd take any who would stand with us.

Raphael's personal guard was hand-selected and bred for one purpose. To decimate any who dared challenge him.

If we entered that building—they very well may succeed in that purpose.

We needed to rain sunlight down them.

"Rose," Frost hissed, and I heard his thoughts imploring me to let Ethan finish this with one press of a button. *She's just one woman,* he thought.

Blake was of a similar mind.

Only Azrael agreed with me, but for an entirely different reason. He wanted to rip his brother apart with his bare hands. He wanted to make it hurt. He wanted Rafe to suffer.

His need for vengeance re-awakened a strength inside me I thought I'd lost after maintaining my compulsion for so long. I straightened, feeling my muscles swell and bulge, taking their place back over my frail bones.

"Take out the windows," I commanded. "All of them."

Ethan grabbed for a chunk of rubble from the road but halted before throwing it as Luz let out a piercing squeal.

My eyes snapped back up to her and an agonized gasp ripped out from my chest.

Luz's squeal trailed off into a soft moan as the metal beam impaling her chest choked off her air supply. Rafe tossed her to the side like trash with a wicked grin on his lips.

The beam caught on something and left her propped up, hanging lip from the metal like a skewered pig.

Bile rose in my throat and numbly, I could feel the guys stepping into my path. I could feel their hands trying to trap me there, knowing that I was about to lose it.

"That won't be necessary," Raphael said, and it took me a minute to realize what he was replying to. He'd heard me tell them to break the windows.

"Blow it!" I screamed, my voice a high, shrill thing that hurt my own ears.

Ethan darted for the phone and jammed the button.

I was pulled sharply back as we all retreated to the next block.

In a blur I saw them come.

As one, Rafe and his minions raced forward to a backdrop of earth-shattering explosions. The *boom* of it rattled in my eardrums, rendering me temporarily deaf. Glass shattered and cement crumbled. The heat blasted against us like a wave.

But carried on its back were a horde of vampires.

Raphael's silhouetted body seemed massive backlit in the deep red glow of flame.

He and his personal guard were outside. Sunlight touched his pale flesh, doing little to subdue the shade of the explosion, but also doing absofuckinglutely nothing to harm him, either.

The others, the vampires who'd retreated from the sun, all burned within the red-hot maw of the crumpling building.

"I'll make this simple," he said, shouting over the roar and yawn of the building coming down behind him. They were barely fifty feet away from us now. If Rafe attacked, he'd be through half of our troop in ten seconds flat.

Blake dragged me out of the way of falling rubble, and together he and the others formed a wall in front of me.

"Hand over the girl and I *won't* kill all of you."

"Like fuck!" Frost bellowed and I wanted to kick him.

You didn't taunt a thousands-of-years-old vampire.

Not unless you wanted to die. Much less a fucking psychopathic one.

"How?" Ethan called across the expanse of smoke-hazed air between us. "How did you do it?"

Rafe raised a brow at him. "Did you really think you were the only soul on this earth smart enough to uncover the secrets hidden in her blood? I've had the best minds at work on it since I got my first taste."

"They won't have much," I said in as low a voice as I could. Rafe hadn't taken enough to be able to test extensively *and* still have some leftover for dosing.

I didn't see any tattoos on them. They must have found another way.

"I'll give you a moment," Rafe called to us, gesturing for his followers to retreat. "But if she doesn't come to me of her own volition..."

He licked his lips and I shuddered.

"I'll be forced to kill all of you."

Rafe turned away, showing us his back as he and his merry band of psychopaths waltzed back toward the building as though the scalding heat of the flames didn't bother them in the slightest.

"We need to run," Ethan urged.

"Fuck that. We need to end this. Here and now."

"If he gets Rose..." Blake trailed off and I slid out of his hold, going to Azrael, the only one who hadn't spoken.

His sights were set on his brother. His body a coil of

clenched muscle and blood-soaked flesh. I tried to read him, but his walls were firmly in pace.

They reminded me, I needed to reinforce my own.

I wondered if he'd come to the same conclusion I had.

That the only way to avoid slaughter was to give myself up.

Except, I couldn't do that.

And judging by the look in Azrael's eyes. He couldn't either.

It's either give you up, or die protecting you, his thoughts flowed out as he gave me a free pass into his mind just for a minute. *I vote neither. Leave my brother to me. If I can end him, his followers will scatter. We just need to kill him.*

His expression turned pained as I slid my hand into his, softening his clenched fist. There was so much more he didn't say, but he didn't have to. He was at war with himself, just as the guys were also at war with each other. Shouting and cursing behind me like a pack of wild dogs.

Azrael couldn't protect me *and* kill his brother. It was one or the other. His thoughts were clear.

"You don't need to protect me."

The sound of my voice silenced all of my guys, leaving only the whispers of our remaining troops to meld with the breathy sounds of reaching flame.

"What you need to do is end this. End him. You're the only one who can."

His eyes glistened and for a terrifying, heart-wrenching second, I thought I was going to be forced to watch him cry. But he held back, shaking his head in a feral snarl. He lifted my hand to his lips and pressed a hard kiss against the back of my palm, smearing blood over my knuckles. *"Live*, my love. *You must live."*

And then he was gone.

18

"*W*hat is he—" Ethan's voice choked off as a resounding *crack!* split the air and my guys realized at the same time I did that the battle had begun. Raphael shot through the air like a round from a cannon, blasted eighty feet toward the sky from Azrael's attack.

There was no time to think after that. They rushed us like a swarm of insects. The sound of the first hit like the pulling of an invisible trigger.

"Stay together!" I yelled, the words drawing out into a war cry as the first of the vampires reached us. I had my katana in one hand and a stake in the other, plucking the last vestiges of energy and strength from my soul.

I wasn't Rose anymore. The blade was an extension of my arm. The stake a sharpened fist. My body was a weapon to be wielded against my enemy. I could feel no pain. No fear. Nothing.

There was no telling how long it went on like that. Surviving on reflex and power of will alone. It could have been a minute. It could have been an hour.

I didn't stop as my muscles began to scream in protest. I didn't stop when my lungs threatened to give out. Or when black spots began to dance in my vision.

There was only the next victim.

There was only kill or be killed.

Until...

"*Fuck*," the pained cry was enough to get through to me. I knew that voice.

I came back to myself all at once, like a rubber band snapping into place. The jarring picture of my reality making me falter just long enough for the vamp at my back to land a hit to my hip that *definitely* cracked bone.

I laid him out a second later, but the damage was done, and I groaned against the stabbing agony in my hip as I searched for the one who'd brought me back.

As I searched for Frost.

My eyes locked on him in a dangerous dance with an opponent, each of them tearing and swiping at one another, trying to get a fatal blow. That wasn't what had me worried, though.

What I couldn't take my eyes off of, even as I felt enemy hands prying my aching body from the black-top, was the steadily growing patch of black as it blossomed over Frost's back, spreading like deadly wings.

Red, raised flesh was appearing elsewhere on his body, too.

The tattoos—they were wearing off.

No.

Not yet.

It was too soon.

I kicked and fought against my attacker, unable to look away from Frost until another cry rang out and the smell of cooking flesh permeated the air.

A vampire fell in a heap of burning flesh to the ground, and another began to succumb.

I found Ethan and Blake. Alive, but they'd begun to burn too.

"Get out of here!" I screeched like a fucking banshee. "Go!"

I clutched the hand dragging me back toward the burning wreckage of Rafe's building and used him as an anchor to stabilize myself as I swung around trapping his legs with mine to bring him down before staking him. My hip felt near splitting, but I ignored it, getting unsteadily to my feet only to fall again, my palms slicing open on the now-jagged road.

I tried to find Azrael in the melee but couldn't see him anywhere. If the guys' tattoos were just now starting to wear off, his would have almost completely lost its effect by now.

I watched, coughing as I inhaled concrete dust and smoke, as Frost dug something out of his pocket and stuffed it into his mouth.

ELENA LAWSON

Blake and Ethan did the same, and it wasn't until I saw the motion of them swallowing that I understood what they had done.

No.

The pills. They'd brought them as a failsafe.

I'd known they were hiding something from me, but this…?

This was suicide.

My eyes burned with unshed, furious, agonized tears.

"Fucking bastards!" I tried to shout but the curse came out as a choked sob.

The pills Ethan had made almost fucking killed Azrael *and* Ethan the last time. It would prolong their ability to withstand the sunlight, but for how much longer?

And when they wore off…

I shuddered.

The rest of our army began to retreat from the daylight, busting through whatever building was nearest to escape their demise.

This was it. After everything, we were going to lose.

We'd all known this was a possibility, but I thought…

Like an *idiot*, I thought good would win out over evil. That's how it always ended in the storybooks, did it not? Good triumphs. Evil falls.

But this was not a fairytale. This was Grimm. This was reality.

Before another of Rafe's minions could get his hands on me, a body barreled into him. Ripping him into three pieces before I could blink.

Azrael.

He was coated in a layer of flaking char, but even burned as he was, there was no mistaking it was him. The pills had kept him from burning alive, too, but they wouldn't save him for long. Soon, he would burn three times as fast, and the burns wouldn't fade in minutes. It would take days. Weeks.

And a *lot* of blood.

"Get out of here!" I screamed.

"Rose!"

I cried out as a sharp pain blasted through my core, making bright stars flare in my vision. The blow to my kidney from behind brought me to my knees and I choked on a sob of agony.

Long fingers twisted in my hair, jerking my head back, scraping my knees over the rubble-coated pavement. I glanced up into the glittering eyes of our enemy and snarled, digging my sharpened fingernails into the flesh of his hand. Trying to tear my head free, uncaring as clumps of hair loosened from my scalp.

Out of the corner of my eye, I saw Azrael brace for attack, but he didn't bolt forward, stopping dead in his tracks as Rafe wrapped his other hand around my throat. He didn't choke me. No.

It was a warning.

He languidly brushed his fingertips over the blood-stained skin there, daring Azrael to move against him.

"Go!" I croaked, panic flaring as Azrael began to burn anew.

The pain was clear, but he didn't budge, letting the sun destroy him inch by inch.

"You look positively awful, brother."

Azrael stepped forward, upper lips curling.

Behind him, I could see the guys barely managing to stay upright as the remainder of Rafe's force descended upon them. Together, the three of them fought off a group of seven and I felt sick, praying with everything inside of me that they were strong enough.

"Now, now, Azrael," Rafe cooed. "Another step and I'll have to snap her pretty neck. I know you don't want that."

"You wouldn't."

"Wouldn't I? It seems her blood cannot be used for the purpose I intended. So, what use do I have for her, brother?"

"Raphael, if you—"

"Are you threatening me? I hardly think that's wise."

Ethan went down a moment later and I gasped, unable to focus on the trouble I was in here stuck between two ancient monsters when my guys were on the brink of their ends not twenty feet away.

Ash rose from his cheek and forearm as a vampire hovered over him, ready to dole out the killing blow.

Stop. I sent the command to the vampire and he

stilled, psychotic gaze twitching this way and that, trying to see where the command came from as he fought it off.

It was harder to bend this one to my will. He was older. Stronger.

But with a little more focus, I had him.

And then I had his friends, too.

It was the reprieve my guys needed to gain the upper hand.

"I see you've learned some new tricks," Rafe's hot breath whispered over my cheek. The reek of his breath made me gag. "Too bad my reinforcements have just arrived."

Reinforcements…?

Crawling like ants from the building across the street from the one that burned, a horde of at least twenty more vampires poured onto the street. But within seconds of their exposure to the light, they began to burn. The burn took them slowly. And with Rafe compulsion poisoning their minds, they wouldn't stop until they were dead. We only needed to fend them off until they couldn't fight anymore.

Rafe had no idea the kind of *tricks* I'd learned... It was time to show him exactly what I could do.

Win or die. Now was the time.

Step one, strengthen mental barriers.

Step two, locate dropped katana. *Got it.*

Step three. Kill a king.

Azrael must've sensed what I was about to do

because his eyes widened infinitesimally in his quickly blackening face the instant before I grabbed Rafe's wrist from my throat, twisting it as I twisted out of his grip until I heard the snapping of bone.

Azrael clashed with him a moment later as I scrambled on hands and knees to my katana, her blade glinting like a beacon in the sunlight.

"We'll hold them off!" I vaguely heard Blake call, his voice a pained growl as my guys raced forward, ready to take on the new force on their own.

Cut the head off the snake.

Cut the head off the snake.

Cut the motherfucking head off the motherfucking snake.

If I could kill Rafe, what remained of the vampires would scatter.

If I could kill Rafe, I might be able to save my guys before it was too late.

Azrael and Rafe clashed in a twist of bodies on the road. All teeth and claws and bulging, sinewy muscle.

Pain scorched down my right leg as I shoved myself to standing, unable to so much as glance in the direction of my guys for fear of what I would see.

Rafe flipped Azrael, straddling his brother as his own flesh began to redden and pucker, scorching in the sun. Azrael took a forceful hit to his face and I winced, plucking up my resolve.

"Don't *fucking* move."

Rafe hesitated for an instant before hitting Azrael

again. His skull knocked forcefully against the pavement.

"I said *stop*."

Rafe's clenched fist shook, and he roared as he broke through my compulsion, hitting Azrael for a third time as I hobbled over, katana dragging against the ground behind me.

I just needed one good swing.

Rafe's eyes snapped up to mine and for once, I didn't shy away from the contact. I didn't try to look away. Because I wasn't the one who would be trapped in his gaze this time.

No.

My mother had been able to compel Rafe, it was the reason she was dead. He couldn't stand living knowing there was a being out there more powerful than him. And she had done it without training. Without a spell cast on her to strengthen her ability.

She compelled Rafe all on her own—to protect *me*.

I let my undeniable *need* to protect my guys wash through me. I cared little what happened to me, but *them?* If there was anything inside of me that was strong enough to beat him, it was my love for them.

It wasn't my rage. Or my fear.

Them.

It had always been them.

The undiluted fear in Rafe's eyes as his body betrayed him, going stiller than a corpse as he remained there, straddling his brother, was the most *delicious* thing I'd ever seen.

I gloated over it for a moment, taking it in as Azrael returned to his senses, shaking his head as a pained croak passed through his lips. On the side of his head, I could see the unmistakable smooth ivory of bone showing through his charred skin.

It was *that* that brought me back to my senses.

I could gloat after he was dead.

But there was one last thing I needed to do real quick before I finished this.

"Get up."

Rafe stood.

Blood poured like a faucet from my nose, but I didn't care.

I jerked down his pants and with a quick slice, had his dick lobbed off. Then his balls, too, just for good measure.

Next went his hands.

My vision waned.

A feral twist of his mouth was the last expression Raphael would ever make as I finally, *finally* took his head.

My consciousness returned in fits and spurts. A barrage of senses attacking from all sides.

I tried to open my eyes but only managed to capture snippets before they would fall back shut.

My guys cried out in pain and I pushed myself hard to awaken. They needed me. I needed to be there for them.

Smoke clogged my nostrils, and my body knew nothing but the dull aching of bone-deep pain and exhaustion. I jerked as someone lifted me, eyes springing open for a moment.

Long enough to see that it was Frost who was carrying me and that the sun was gone. No, not gone. We'd simply passed into shadow. We were inside a building, hidden away from the light.

Frost. Frost was alive.

What about the others?

"Rosie," he implored me, his voice hoarse. I took in the state of him, seeing that his neck was burned all the way through skin and muscle. At once I realized how the arms holding me up were shaking. "Rosie, wake up."

My head lolled back, and I saw Ethan and Blake dragging an unconscious Azrael through busted double doors behind us. My heart sang and broke all at once. They were alive, yes, but their injuries were so severe I had to wonder for how long?

Beyond them, a battle raged on. Colorful sparks burst in the air like fireworks. Strange words rose like broken music as, I struggled to understand what I was seeing.

"W-witches?" I stammered, trying to lift my head as Frost's legs buckled beneath him and he slammed down to one knee, coughing until blood stained his lips.

The others caught up, forming a circle around Frost and me as they, too, succumbed to their injuries, sprawling over the floor in heaps. Ethan could hardly breathe. Blake's face was twisted as he clutched an arm to his chest that was mostly bone.

My heart shattered.

It didn't matter to me that Rafe was dead anymore.

I'd raise him back from the depths of hell myself if it meant I could save them. I'd go with him. I'd do whatever he wanted. I should have done just that. I should have let the world burn to save them.

I could've saved them.

"Drink," I croaked, flooding my voice with compulsion.

I was weak, but I was quickly regaining my strength. They were not.

And they would not unless they took what they needed from me. We'd stupidly cleared the entire area of humans. I was their only option for survival.

Frost's grip on me tightened as he resisted.

Their thoughts were discordant, but there was a common thread. Resistance.

I was going to have to work harder if I wanted them to live.

Planting my hands on Frost's chest I pushed off from him and he fell back, barely able to hold himself in a seated potion as I crawled so I was between them all.

I prodded Azrael, lifting his head into my lap with a grimace as I felt skin pull away from bone. I snatched a shard of glass from the floor and sliced into my thigh, pressing his face into the wound.

"*Drink,*" I demanded.

"*Drink,*" I repeated through gritted teeth, willing my lingering strength to be enough to compel him.

"All of you," I added, meeting each set of terrified eyes around me. "Drink."

"Rose, we can't—"

"Shut up and do it."

Azrael's fangs sank into my thigh first and a whistle of a breath pushed out through my teeth as euphoria mixed with all the other emotions wreaking havoc within.

Blake dragged himself nearer on his belly, tiny curses spilling from his lips as he came.

Frost looked as though he were ready to chew off his own arms if only to stop himself.

And Ethan...Ethan, barely able to draw a breath, fought every inch as his head leaned in without his permission.

Please, I could hear in his mind. *Please don't do this.*

You'll die.

This is suicide.

"But you'll live," I replied in a whisper as Blake's mouth closed around my wrist and Frost's resistance broke with a snarl as he savagely bit down into the muscle where my shoulder connected with my neck.

Ethan was the last to submit, but with a last push of my compulsion, latched onto his eyes, he did as he was told.

They were, all of them, too weak to deny me.

Even Azrael was powerless to stop feeding.

They would need every drop if they had even the smallest hope of surviving their injuries. Even then, they would remain here, writhing on the floor for days or longer before they would be able to move. But they would be *alive.*

They could rule the vampires alongside Azrael. I was confident they would do it in the way I'd envisioned and there was nothing more I could ask of them.

We'd done what we set out to do. Against all odds, Rafe was dead. My life was a fair trade for that victory.

One day, they'd forgive me.

I couldn't imagine the alternative.

I sank deep into the pleasurable euphoria of their venom, letting it gallop through my veins like a band of wild horses. I rode on its back, writhing and moaning, coming apart at the seams.

If ever there was a perfect way to go, this was it.

The pain forgotten.

The world falling away.

My eyelids peeled back as my eyes rolled into my skull, back arching from the floor as my heartbeat began to slow. I could feel the change as it happened. I could hear my guys screaming inside their heads, but I tuned them out, choosing to focus instead on the thudding in my chest as it began to stutter, evening out into a broken rhythm of distantly interspersed thuds.

A garbled voice above us drew my attention and I found I was able to open my eyes enough to see her.

Amala.

Her dark skin unmarred, she looked like an angel instead of a witch as she stared down at me, a look of disgust crossing her face.

"It isn't your time."

Amala bent at the waist and her deep plum robe brushed against my cheek where I lay immobile against the cool tile. Her outstretched hands took hold of my face, her fingers soft as silk.

"S-save them…"

"No, child. I'm saving you."

With a flick of her wrists, my neck snapped. I felt the disconnect from spine to skull and had just enough time to realize what she'd done before the light faded from my eyes and there was only darkness.

20

A sweet aroma roused me. I could feel the nearness of a beating heart that was not my own. My throat ached as though clogged with razor-blades and my chest pinched with a tightness, I could not seem to shake no matter how hard I tried to draw deep breath to clear it.

Movement behind my eyelids.

An attacker.

I shot forward, awake at once with a burning in my chest as I throttled the one who dared try to kill me while I was unconscious. Black spots crowded my vision and I worked to cast them away, my hand gripped tightly around the soft skin of a throat.

A feral hiss rose from my right and I jerked to the side, checking for another attacker with limited vision only to realize the sound hadn't come from my side. It had come from me.

"Rose!" The sharp screech cleared my mind long enough for me to realize that my hand was wrapped around the throat of someone *living*.

There had been a beating heart.

The woman struggling against my suffocating grip spluttered wriggled, trying to get free. As her face became clear my stomach soured.

I pried my clenched hand from her neck and Estelle slumped to the ground coughing and gagging, trying to get her breath.

Someone knelt to help her, and I recognized their scent.

Their *scent*?

It was Valentina.

Estelle shoved her helping hands away and stood shakily to her feet, eyeing me with a fear in her eyes that I didn't think I'd ever seen there before.

"I-I'm sorry," I tried to say, but my voice was a dry, cracked, whisper and I worked to wet the intense dryness in my throat. It felt like trying to swallow sand.

"That's alright dear," Estelle replied, her own voice sounding just as strangled now as my own. "I'll just be going then."

My body heated, with embarrassment maybe? But suddenly, I was so fucking hot I couldn't stand it and a discomfited moan came unbidden from my lips as I searched for something cold.

"Ice," I croaked. "Can someone get me some ice?"

I heard Valentina whisper a command to someone

and lifted my gaze to find her standing awkwardly at the center of the room.

The room, I recognized it. It took my slow mind a few seconds to put it together that we were back in Italy. Back at Azrael's mansion. And the couch where I'd been laying was the same one Valentina had lain dead on barely a month ago.

There were three males at her back. Her harem. Much smaller now than it had been. One of them left for the ice she requested, and she watched him leave with a bereft look in her eyes. My heart ached for her.

I wouldn't want them out of my sight either.

Wait…

"Where are they?" I demanded, rubbing my sore throat with oddly clean fingers.

Hadn't they been bloody?

Hadn't I been falling apart?

Should I not be dead?

"They're recovering."

My head turned so swiftly to my left that I gave myself whiplash. "Amala?"

Her head cocked to one side as she appraised me not so differently than one would appraise a prized horse or a particularly large bet.

It came back to me like a bolt of white-hot lightning. The fight in the streets of New York city. Rafe's head detached from his body. My guys barely alive.

And the witches… fighting against what remained

ELENA LAWSON

of the vampires outside while I worked to save my guys.

"You killed me," I breathed, spluttering as a rib-aching cough took me and I searched the immediate area for water.

"They want to follow *you*," Amala replied plainly. "You can control them, but only so long as you *live*."

My blood grew cold in my veins and I looked within, feeling the monumental shift in my being, as though my soul itself had moved. My heart was beating, but there was a difference in the pace of it. My body was healed entirely of its wounds. I'd *scented* Valentina before I'd seen her. I'd *smelled* Estelle's blood.

The sweet memory of it made my mouth water.

I almost vomited.

"I'm transitioning," I said, the words barely above a whisper, mostly for myself.

"Yes," Amala confirmed.

"I may not survive the transition," I replied through gritted teeth, my fingers tearing out entire chunks of sofa before I could rein myself in. I chucked the foamy pierces to the floor and took a long breath, realizing how strange it felt. How my lungs almost wanted to reject the airflow.

"A worthwhile risk."

Amala strolled casually to the armchair opposite me and swanned into it, lifting her deep plum robes as she sat. "You were on the verge of death. If I'd let them feed from you for another moment or even if I'd have stopped them, you'd have died."

"I was prepared for that!"

She shook her head. "You're strong, Rose. I have every confidence you'll survive to see yourself remade immortal. And then I have every confidence that you'll come to be a *just* ruler."

"Why did you help us?" I wondered. "You said you wouldn't get involved, but I saw you. I saw the witches taking out the rest of Rafe's army."

"Once he was dead there was no risk in helping to clean up the rest of the *mess*."

I laughed and the sound was crazed even to my own ears.

"I get it, you had us do all the hard work and then you just...get to reap the rewards."

She didn't disagree with me, merely stared, her ancient gaze passing over every inch of my face as though searching for weak points. She was trying to assess whether or not I would survive this. She wasn't as confident as she originally let on.

I tried to push into her thoughts but was met with a solid shove.

"I'm afraid you won't be strong enough for that until the transition is complete."

I seethed to myself for a moment until something else she said sank in and my lips parted, a weight lifting free in my gut. "You said they're recovering?"

I didn't need to explain who.

267

"They're alive? All of them?"

I braced for world-ending agony as Amala took her time responding.

"It seems your actions back in New York were enough to keep them from the true death for now. They have a long road to recovery. It will be days. Maybe a week of regular feeding and rest before they'll heal."

"And the girls?"

How long had I been unconscious? Were they alright? Were they still in police custody? They were free and I took solace in that, but it wasn't enough, they deserved more than a shaky start.

"I grew fond of them during my time with Raphael," Amala replied. "They were brought with us and are making use of the bathhouse and adjoining quarters on the other end of the property.

I hadn't even known there was a bathhouse here, but it didn't shock me.

"What remains of your...*army*...is also on the premises. They await your command once you are ready to give it."

I hadn't the heart to ask how many survived. Judging by the look on Valentina's face, I had to assume it wasn't good.

"I'm so sorry Val."

"We knew what we were signing up for."

One of her mates took her by the hand and she melded into his side. I could sense how the strength flowed between them. Not two separate beings anymore, but two parts of a whole.

As though reading my next thoughts, Val cleared her throat and spoke again. "They're all still loyal even though..." she trailed off.

"Even though I can't give them the sun anymore."

"We don't know that for certain," Amala said. "Though I suspect that will be the case."

She didn't seem the least bit sorry for that fact. Actually, she seemed almost exultant, and I realized at once that she—and the rest—of the witches would like that our race was confined to the nighttime hours. That we could only wreak havoc after the sun sets.

Yet another reason why she ended me no doubt. Two birds, one dead Rose.

All her problems solved.

We played into her hand beautifully.

I let the knowledge Rafe was dead erase all the other uncertainties from my mind. I could worry about the politics later. For now, I would revel in the fact that I'd killed my enemy, I'd saved my men, and I would live to see them at least one more time if I didn't survive the transition.

It was all more than I could've hoped for and fresh tears welled in my eyes. *We did it.*

"I want to see them. I need to see they're alright."

I moved to stand just as one of Val's blood-mates returned, empty-handed. "Sorry, no ice."

Oddly, I wasn't so hot anymore anyway. In fact, I

ELENA LAWSON

was a bit chilly and strange clammy sweat clung to my chest.

"The rushed menopause really fucking blows," Valentina offered with a wincing shrug and I groaned, rising to my feet a little unsteadily.

Right. I'd forgotten about that part.

Great.

Menopause in my twenties. Every girl's dream.

"Not so fast." Val came forward to stabilize me, pinning me in place with a look. "If you're going to make it through this then you need to feed."

She must've seen the look on my face because her gaze softened, and an understanding settled between us. "Trust me. Once you get past the first few swallows, you'll be begging me for more."

Oh god.

One of Valentina's mates passed her a blood bag from a cooler on the floor and she pressed it into my chest, forcing me to take it. "Do it for *them*."

I didn't think I'd have taken it from her if she'd said anything else. But those four words were enough to push me to close my shaky fingers over the cool plastic and grip the plastic stopper with my teeth. I popped it off and spat it to the carpet, not allowing myself a moment's hesitation, afraid if I did, I'd toss the bag away and run. I'd run and not look back.

Do it for them.

I pulled forcefully, drawing the thick nectar into my mouth. I gagged on the syrupy thickness after the first

270

gulp, but as I felt it carve a path down my throat and spiderweb out to my extremities, I found myself oddly entranced. Greedy fingers kneaded the plastic bag, helping to drain the liquid into my mouth faster. I cried out as I finished it, huffing, head spinning.

Pain.

I lifted my fingers to my gums, snatching them back when the gentle pressure radiated a deep throbbing pain through my entire jaw. Two identical bumps were forming above my canines and I ran over them with my tongue. Equal parts horrified and in awe.

I dragged my finger lazily through Blake's hair, reveling in its softness. Part of the left side of his head had burned so severely that the hair there still hadn't grown back, but pinkish flesh proved that he was in-fact healing. I had no doubt the hair would grow back too.

"He'll wake up soon, Rosie," Frost's throaty rumble sounded behind me and I reached backward, feeling for him. He took my hand and tucked it to his chest as he sat beside me. His weight on the mattress so much more than mine that I fell back into him, sighing as he wrapped his arms around me.

It had taken Ethan and Frost two and a half days to wake up. I'd been unconscious for two days before that. But both Blake and Azrael still had yet to open their eyes.

Without a beating heart, it was hard not to think

they may not wake at all, but each day we were reassured by small improvements in their physical healing.

Wounds closed. Skin that was black with char began to build over with fresh pink skin. Muscle knitted back together. Fresh baby hairs cropped up.

All we could do was wait to see if they would wake.

"You should lay back down," I urged Frost, but it was hard to sound commanding about it. The truth was, I barely let either of my men out of my sight since they woke up. I'd banned them from leaving this room and had effectively locked myself inside of it with them, only leaving twice a day to check on Azrael downstairs in his chambers.

I'd wanted to have him moved up here to our room where he belonged, but with all the separate beds and vampire staff coming in and out to clean wounds and re-fill IV's with fresh blood bags, there wasn't the space.

I found it near impossible to stand being around Estelle and the one other mortal woman who helped her in the kitchens. So much so that I'd sent them away to stay in the bathhouse with the girls. We didn't need kitchen staff here anymore, anyway. There was no one to eat anything aside from blood, and I could see some of the vampires wandering about looking at Estelle and the other one with hunger in their eyes.

It wasn't safe to keep them here, as much as I wished I could enjoy her chicken soup, I didn't think I would ever be able to enjoy the taste again. She made meatballs the day before yesterday and just the smell of them nearly had me vomiting everywhere.

I sighed again and Frost pressed his hand to my back, lifting my shirt slightly to feel my weak pulse through my skin. Something he'd been doing every so often since he woke up. At least Ethan had listened when I told him to stay laying down. Frost was another story though.

He dragged his IV around the room with him, following me even to the bathroom. Like he was afraid if he stopped watching me, I would drop dead and he wouldn't be there to stop it.

Not like he could do a damn thing if the transition claimed me anyway.

"It's getting weaker," he grunted.

"Is she okay?" Ethan asked, waking at the sound of our conversation.

"I'm fine," I reassured them both, though I didn't feel it.

"Hey!" Frost barked and immediately a face popped into the doorway, glancing between Frost and I on the bed next to Blake. "Get her some more blood."

The vampire gave a nod and raced off to do Frost's bidding.

"I think a weakened heartbeat is kind of the point, isn't it?" I asked, going for a light tone but the words only managed to sound weak.

He pressed his forehead against the back of my head and a gush of hot breath whispered over the back of my neck, making me shiver. If I wasn't still so weak. If *they* weren't still so weak, that alone would have had me creaming my panties.

"When it stops, you could die."

"Or I could go on living. Or...*un*living? Animated but dead? Not really sure how to word that."

"Quit being a smart-ass."

I shrugged.

"It's all I got left. Don't take it from me."

He pressed his lips to my hair and pulled back.

A moment later, the vampire returned with not one, but *two* fresh blood bags. I didn't bother asking where they were getting them from. Either Azrael had a store of them or one of them had a connection we didn't know about. It kept coming, and that was all that mattered right now.

"Thank you," I said, tipping my head as the male vampire bowed, passing me the bags. "I want you to set up a faster drip for Blake. Azrael, too. One bag every hour on the hour."

"Isn't that a little excessive?" Frost asked and I cut him a glare that dared him to argue before turning my attention back to the other vampire. I thought his name was Draven.

"Do it," I told him. "And monitor Azrael for signs of change. Report back to me immediately if you notice anything or if he wakes. I'll be down to check on him myself in an hour."

Draven nodded. "Yes, my queen."

. . .

IT WAS another day before I felt ready to leave my guys, even for a minute, but being inside so long was starting to wear on me. I found I was already super sensitive to sunlight, even if it didn't immediately burn yet, so I had to wait until nightfall to go outside.

Blake woke up seven hours ago, after I'd had them all on the regiment of a full blood bag every hour. Their recovery time was improving vastly. Frost had removed his IV already and was giving out orders to the vampires waiting for them. Ethan was already back in the lab, tinkering away with a new sample of my blood.

Disappointingly, Amala had been right. My blood would no longer produce any sort of *vampire sunblock,* but Ethan still maintained that it showed vast differences to regular vampire blood and he thought it could be useful for other purposes. He seemed genuinely excited to find out what.

Blake was back asleep, but he was nearing the point of being able to stop the blood treatment now too.

I didn't want to tell them before I left to go outside alone, insisting that I needed a moment of solace, but I could feel it coming on.

All day I'd had to stop and check to make sure my heart still beat. I kept thinking it was over. That it'd finally stopped, and I'd lived. Then it would beat again. Sometimes once and then not again for nearly ten

ELENA LAWSON

seconds. Sometimes several times in a row and then not for nearly twenty.

I felt faint and sweaty.

As I took in a breath of the flower-scented air outside the estate, admiring the gentle curve of the crescent moon hanging in the navy sky as I found a place to be alone.

I could smell fresh blood on the breeze and could immediately tell that the bathhouse was somewhere east, likely hidden by the tangle of tall bushes along the edges of the front lawn. I ignored my thirst, shoving the urge to feed down deep inside of me.

I'd just had two blood bags for dinner for fuck's sake. How much more could I possibly ingest?

I didn't think I'd ever fault a newborn vamp for losing control ever again. In fact, I'd already come up with a plan to offer a safe haven for the newly turned, so they could learn self-control away from fragile mortals.

If they chose not to take the generous offer, then what they did would be on their heads.

I cast the thoughts away. Politics later.

Right now, I had to focus on not fucking dying.

My heart beat hard, a single thud that was so forceful it made me gasp. I trapped the sound between my lips, though. I couldn't risk the guys coming out here right now.

I wouldn't allow them to watch me die if that was how this was going to go down.

If I was going to die, I was going to do it here, alone, with only the moon as witness.

The next beat came nearly thirty seconds later and this one shook my entire body until I fell onto my side, face grating against the gritty stone steps of the mansion.

My cheeks hollowed as I held my breath against a lancing pain through my chest, seeing stars in my eyes.

Please.

A tingle raced down my spine and my body convulsed with the next beat, this time rending me unable to hold back a choked gasp at the tension.

Please.

Light spilled onto the steps and the panic spurred by a foreign voice shouting sent me tumbling into full-body spasms. Something clogged my throat and I felt three sets of hands embracing me. Prodding me. Lifting me.

Their words were lost to my delirium and I nearly bit off my tongue as my body moved back into the light and my back pressed into something hard as hands held me down. Held me still. Held my head to one side.

Pressure.

Pressure everywhere.

And then no more as the spasming stopped and my eyes rolled back to forward, and the cotton fell from my ears.

"Rose?"

"Rosie, are you with us?"

ELENA LAWSON

"Fuck, Rose, say something!"

I blinked, a hand going to my chest. It was still. Absolutely and perfectly still. And yet I could move. I could think.

I *am*.

"Well, that fucking sucked," I muttered, my voice a watery mess as tears spilled over and rolled down my temples to the floor.

They piled onto me, burying wet faces into my neck, stomach, and side. I held them to me, trembling uncontrollably.

I survived it.

I'd become the one thing I once would have rather died than become.

I couldn't be fucking happier.

"Looks like you fuckers are stuck with me," I sobbed. "*Literally* forever."

"I can't think of a better place to be stuck," Ethan said, laying a kiss on my cheek.

I met his golden eyes and broke into a wide smile.

"The fangs suit you," he said, swiping at his eyes with the back of his hand. "Sexy as fuck."

I reached up and felt the sharp points, cutting the tip of my finger by accident. Blake took the digit into his mouth, suckling gently. My core tightened at the sensation and my pussy instantly wetted.

His dark gaze washed over my face. "Ours."

"*Mine*," I hissed back.

"What's that?" Frost asked, and I turned to find his

brows drawn together. Head tipped to one side as though he could hear something we could not.

The sound of keys being expertly stroked on a piano struck a much deeper chord within me. *Azrael.*

As one, all four of us wandered past the curious stares of the vampires crowding around to witness my transformation. They bowed as we passed them, our minds moving as one with our bodies.

I could hear them now. The thoughts of guys and everyone else within a several mile radius, I thought. It was as easy as tuning a radio and picturing it as such helped me to shut down the stations I didn't need to hear right then, zeroing in on the one mind I needed to hear.

Azrael's.

His mind was filled with a symphony of thought, crashing, and rising with each stroke of the keys at his fingertips as we made our way down, deep into the cavernous room where he waited below.

My guys filed into the cool chamber behind me and we stopped to watch as Azrael played, enraptured by the tune. It was the one he played for me in New York the night before the battle.

Requiem for a Rose.

The fire blazing in the hearth played with the shadows and light over his naked body, revealing how much he'd healed, and how much he still needed to.

Small burn marks around his ankles and on the back of one of his arms were still an angry red, but all of his other injuries seemed gone entirely. The smooth plane of his back made my fingers ache to touch him. I had to be sure he was real. Alive.

That this wasn't an elaborate concoction of my mind. Hell, maybe I *had* died upstairs, and this was my heaven. All of my males, alive. Whole. It was the closest thing to eternal bliss anyone could ever get.

The tension drained from his shoulders as the last note hovered in the air of the cavernous room. Unable to help myself any longer, I crossed the space to him, sliding my hands down his bare chest, nuzzling the spot behind his ear.

His music was hypnotic, as evidenced by the fact that the rest of my guys were staring slack-jawed behind me. Azrael turned his head and met my lips with his; a soft, sweet kiss.

He pulled away only for a moment, marveling at me as though he held a prized diamond in his hands instead of a withering Rose. Like he always knew I'd make the most incredible vampire.

Without looking, I held out my hand behind me and felt Frost's huge hand slide into mine. They were all still healing, but they needed me as much as I needed them. I pulled him close and he wrapped his arms around me, moving my hair out of the way to press light kisses to my shoulder and neck. He didn't protest or balk at Azrael's open affection, which was promising.

It gave me hope that I could still have everything, despite what I'd lost.

And who I'd almost lost.

Frost reached up and buried his hand in Azrael's russet hair. Two pairs of eyes glanced at me, Frost's icy blues and Az's mismatched set, then Frost drew him close, hesitating for only a second before their lips met. He was asking Azrael's forgiveness for his former hostility, asking me to forgive his selfishness.

Dumbass. I'd already forgiven him for that.

But the sight of them made a new kind of hunger stir in my belly. Azrael returned the kiss eagerly, breaking off only when I tugged at the two of them. I gave them my best temptress smile and pulled my shirt over my head slowly, moving toward the bed where Ethan already waited. Blake stood nearby, arms crossed and smirking as he watched the scene unfold.

The very idea of having all four of them nearly had me cumming in my pants.

"I have all my pieces here," I purred, tracing a finger across Ethan's jaw. I turned back to the other three and popped the button on my pants. "Now let's see how many different ways this puzzle fits together."

Frost's eyes sparkled in the firelight and he pushed Azrael toward me. "Looks like she needs help getting undressed. Why don't you and Ethan get her ready?"

Warmth flooded my chest at his consideration, but then blue and brown eyes settled on me and my mouth went dry. He didn't hesitate at the invitation, his erection already at half-mast. Ethan's breath stirred the hair on top of my head as he reached around and unzipped my pants. Then his strong arms lifted me while Az knelt and pulled them off, exposing me to the cool air of the cavern.

I could feel the steel length of Ethan's mammoth cock pressing into my back, but Azrael held my attention with soft kisses up my leg. I squirmed in Ethan's grip, throwing my head back on his shoulder when Azrael's tongue dipped into my sex. Ethan nuzzled me, planting equally soft kisses on my temple, my cheek, my neck. They were teaming up on the tender side and it wasn't fair.

Pressure on my nipple made my eyes snap open to find that Blake had joined us, shirt off, pants undone. He rolled my perky nipple in his mouth, tongue swirling. I wanted to touch someone, but Ethan had my arms clamped down tight to my sides. Frost leaned against the piano, half undressed like Blake, palming his hard-on as he watched.

Holy fuck, it was hot in here.

My core tightened with each flick of Azrael's tongue, his maddeningly slow torture complimenting Blake's attention and Ethan's tight hold. Blake released my nipple with a soft pop and kicked away his pants. I licked my lips, realizing belatedly that my fangs had extended.

That was really going to take some getting used to.

"Looks like someone's ready to do the biting this time," Blake commented.

"Who do you want first, my queen?" Ethan whispered in my ear.

Without thinking, my eyes locked onto Frost. He'd always been my first in all the ways that mattered to me. Even with my head foggy with lust, he was the one. His pants fell to the floor and he approached, nodding to Ethan.

"Put her on the bed."

The commanding tone sent a pleasurable jolt through my system. I was loathe to leave Azrael's skillful tongue, but my body was on autopilot. My little minx had more than one desire now, and she wanted Frost's blood, wanted to see him writhe under the effects of the venom I now had.

She wanted control.

Or maybe that was all me.

As soon as Frost crawled onto the bed with me, I circled my finger, indicating for him to turn around. His brow drew down in confusion, but he did as told. He didn't give up command in the bedroom lightly, but I knew he wouldn't refuse me. I pressed myself against his back, running my hand up his arm, across the smooth skin of his shoulder and neck, and up into his white-blonde hair. He tilted his head obediently.

"So many possibilities." I eyed the three standing by the bed and smiled. Since he'd been the one holding me, Ethan was the only one still dressed. "I think Ethan needs help getting out of his clothes. Do you mind? Slowly, now."

With my hand in his short hair, I turned Frost's head to watch with me through half-lidded eyes. Blake ran his hands up Ethan's tight stomach, pulling his shirt over his head, while Az slid his hands around Ethan's hips to undo his pants. Az really knew how to play the game, making Ethan respond to his sensual touch, pressing back against him. Silky wetness coated my thighs as I pictured all the ways I wanted to have them, all the ways I wanted them to have each other.

Blake grinned, dark eyes burning through me. "Mm, I like this Rose."

"Oh, this is the same Rose," Az said, matching Blake's expression. "She just kicked down her walls."

"This Rose wants all of you up here with her." I crooked my finger at them. "Together."

Azrael was the first to move, taking position behind me after planting a lingering kiss on my lips. Ethan and Blake shared a look and a nod, following Azrael's lead with a kiss before taking up positions that made my mouth water. Ethan laid on his back with his head under Frost's cock and started stroking it while Blake settled between Ethan's knees.

I was so fucking wet just from watching that Azrael had no trouble easing himself inside me. Frost grunted as Ethan swallowed him and I clung to his shoulders, partly to watch and partly to steady myself against Az's slow thrusts. Ethan echoed that noise when Blake entered him, and I scraped my fangs on Frost's shoulder, ready to bite down.

"Wait for it, Rosie."

I didn't. I couldn't.

I bit.

Frost gasped as my fangs pierced his flesh, groaning as my venom flooded his senses. It was weird to think of how fucking delicious he was. My left arm wrapped across his chest, the other holding his throat lightly, forcing his chin up and to the side. I had to remind myself of my newfound strength, so I didn't crush him. He folded his fingers into mine, his other hand covering one of Ethan's where he had a firm grip on Frost's hips.

The power surging through me, in combination with Azrael's slow fucking, had me ready to burst.

I pulled back, licking at the blood welling up as the wound started to close, then held him tighter to me. As soon as my fangs were clear, Az picked his pace up considerably. The sound of my moans echoed through the chamber, seeming to spur the other guys on as well. Through the haze, I watched Blake stroke Ethan as he rammed into him. Ethan moaned around Frost's dick, making Frost curse under his breath.

Azrael's breath brushed across my shoulder a second before I was lost to the pull of his venom, body tingling with the rush. I hadn't been sure how much it would affect me, being one of them now, but the effect was only slightly diminished. Still powerful enough to enjoy. To crave.

But I wanted more.

As much as I loved watching my guys together, I needed to be in there with them, in the middle of them. Az released me, my thought projecting to him. I circled around Frost, tugging Az into my spot behind him, and straddled Ethan, lowering myself on his giant cock reverse cowgirl-style. That put me face-to-face with Blake and his savage smile.

My arms snaked around his neck, his overlapping Ethan's on my hips, and he didn't even flinch when my fingertips brushed across the top of his back. His tongue plunged into my mouth as he and Ethan timed their thrusts with each other. I bit gently on his bottom lip, my fucking fangs getting in the way again. His dark eyes met mine and, beneath the lustful glaze, was an abundance of trust and love.

"Go ahead, Rose," he said quietly.

He knew I wanted to bite all of them. Mark them as mine, even though they would heal. I glanced back to find Azrael having a go at Frost in my absence, which was fucking hot. Blake tilted his head to the side, exposing his beautiful neck, and I didn't hesitate. I latched on, the taste of him filling my mouth, warming my body in a wholly different way than Ethan's hard cock was. A short exhalation was his only reaction, though I could feel the effects in his muscles. His pace picked up, his end drawing near, I knew.

I grabbed his face, meeting his eyes. "Don't cum until I say so."

He growled and I grinned, my gaze dipping to his luscious lips before taking them again. I wasn't sure if I could hold out that long myself in the midst of all this. But I still had Ethan and Az to mark, and I had to try.

"I'm gonna turn around," I told Blake. "I want you both."

Blake pulled himself from Ethan and I turned, sliding my hands up Ethan's chest as Blake worked into my ass. My breaths came in short gasps as they filled me, one pulling out while the other pushed in, faster and faster. I leaned onto Ethan's chest, but I couldn't quite reach that sweet spot on his shoulder or neck. So, I grabbed his hand where he held my waist, pulled it to my mouth, and bit into the inside of his wrist.

Ethan groaned and bucked, hitting a spot so deep I was seeing stars. I cried out around his wrist, knowing my end was closing in on me. A hand swept up my cheek and I released Ethan to find a very drugged Frost watching me. I smirked and leaned down onto Ethan, tugging Frost's cock from his mouth to take for myself.

If Frost was lost in ecstasy before, that was nothing compared to how he reacted when Ethan started working on his balls. Frost's huge hands fisted in my hair, thrusting into my mouth almost as hard as Ethan and Blake were in my pussy and ass.

I was a mess of sensation, on the verge of imploding. My entire being was vibrating with the need for release. I reached back with one hand and touched Blake's, a silent message.

Cum for me.

Blake huffed a short breath, not arguing, just doing. His powerful thrusts drove me over the edge, my insides squeezing down on Ethan and bringing him along for the ride. I moaned as I shattered into a thousand tiny pieces and salty hot liquid splashed the back of my throat. Frost made a manly whimpering sound and I heard Az grunt behind him.

Like a chain fucking reaction.

Oh, but I wasn't nearly done with these guys yet.

One of the advantages to being a vampire: stamina.

I gave myself a moment to come down from my intense fucking orgasm, wondering whether or not it was just my vampire senses that made it all seem more. Then I went for Azrael.

At least I tried, until Blake caught my ankle. I whipped my head back to glare at him for interrupting my plans.

"Wouldn't you like to give us a chance to share the new toy?" he asked, eyes flicking to where Frost was now pinned between Azrael and Ethan.

Azrael gave us the side-eye and a smirk that exposed one fang. I shuddered. I wanted in that sandwich. Frost latched onto Ethan's neck, pressing him close enough to rub their erections together.

I looked back at Blake and cocked a curious eyebrow. "What did you have in mind?"

There was a moment of hesitation, which surprised the hell out of me, then he pulled me close and kissed me. "Follow my lead."

An image popped into my head that had my stomach tying itself into knots. When I turned to face the others again, Azrael was eyeing Blake wickedly. He gently separated Frost and Ethan, both sufficiently dosed with venom, and laid on his back. Blake set himself up to enter Az—I was practically purring at the sight—and Frost was at Azrael's head. Ethan looked unsure of himself even as Blake pulled him around behind him.

Fuck. Blake hated people seeing or touching his back, but he'd just let Ethan... My chest swelled watching them, excited to see how they all grew into each other, pushed each other. How we'd all evolve together over our endless years.

Then Azrael crooked his finger at me and gestured around his face.

Oh.

I was on him in a split second, his tongue delving into my sex. Frost's hands gripped my hips as he positioned himself at my entrance. In front of me, Blake's muscles were tense as Ethan settled behind him. I reached out and threaded my fingers into his, pushing all the love I had for him through that small connection. Ethan's hand snaked around and met ours, pulsing with the same vibes, and Blake relaxed bit by bit.

I fucking loved these guys.

All of them.

Frost thrust into me and everything devolved into glorious, unrepentant chaos. My core twisted and writhed as Azrael and Frost unleashed all they had on me. I pumped Azrael's cock with my hand and sunk my fangs into his thigh, marking him, moaning as he mirrored the action on mine. Another dose of venom coursed through me, dizzying, delightful.

More.

More.

I licked the spot as I pulled away, glancing up at the hitch in Blake's breath to find Ethan on his neck. Fucking chaos. Oblivion approached and I braced to meet it head-on. Azrael's cock slid down my throat and he thrust, wrapping his arms around my thighs to spread my cheeks. My chest tightened, the promise of sweet release just beyond my reach.

I was a tightrope ready to snap.

Blake's fingers found my hair and held on, breaths growing short and erratic as he pounded into Azrael, as Ethan did him. All five of us were connected, all together, all one. The reality of that, of seeing us all come together so easily, hit me all at once.

That was what undid me.

The world went white for a few moments as every single nerve lit up like fucking Independence Day. My eyes watered with the sheer force of it and heat washed down my throat as I took Az with me. The glorious sounds of orgasms bounced off the walls, from me, from the guys. My guys.

My puzzle of souls was complete.

But we weren't four anymore.

We were five.

Printed in Great Britain
by Amazon